JOHN CUNLIFFE'S
DRAGON
STORIES

John Cunliffe's
DRAGON
STORIES

Illustrated by
Alex Pendle

Hippo

For Sylvia and Julian

Scholastic Children's Books,
Scholastic Publications Ltd,
7-9 Pratt Street, London NW1 0AE

Scholastic Inc.,
555 Broadway, New York, NY 10012-3999, USA

Scholastic Canada Ltd,
123 Newkirk Road, Richmond Hill,
Ontario, Canada L4C 4G5

Ashton Scholastic Pty Ltd,
PO Box 579, Gosford, New South Wales,
Australia

Ashton Scholastic Ltd,
Private Bag 92801, Penrose, Auckland,
New Zealand

First published by André Deutsch as THE GREAT DRAGON COMPETITION
AND OTHER STORIES, 1973
First published in this edition by Scholastic Publications Ltd, 1994

Copyright © John Cunliffe 1973 and 1994

ISBN 0 590 55718 1

Printed by Cox & Wyman Ltd, Reading, Berks.

CONTENTS

One
Sir Madoc and the transmogrified dragon 7

Two
Good medicine for a dragon 21

Three
The great dragon competition 33

Four
The Rottingdean dragon 48

Five
A race with a dragon 61

Six
*The man who asked questions and
how he met a dragon* 72

Seven
Sylvia and the dragon 89

Eight
King Calamy and the dragon's egg 110

Nine
Inside outside 123

Ten
The very greedy monster 137

One

Sir Madoc and the transmogrified dragon

A brave knight rode out to fight a dragon, and as he rode he thought that this was the strangest dragon he had ever faced; for the king had taken Sir Madoc aside (that was the knight's name) and warned him: 'This is no ordinary dragon that troubles us. He has magical powers and because of this has killed many good warriors who have gone to meet him. You see, he can change his shape into whatever he pleases. From moment to moment, he can become eagle or poisonous snake; bear, leopard or tiger; fierce elephant or fatal spider; secret mouse or mole beneath the earth. There is no shape that he cannot take.'

'Is there no limit to this beast's magical powers?' asked Sir Madoc.

'Only one,' replied the king. 'There is an ancient prophecy, spoken in past ages by a witch of this country, that the dragon would one day take on a shape that would become his for all time; he would never again be able to change.

Perhaps it is the one shape he has never tried that will be fatal for him; perhaps it is a day when the stars are set against him. No one can tell. You must trust to fortune, and be wary at all times, and watch for any beast that may attack you, be it in the sky, or on the earth, or under the very ground you stand on.

'A dreadful creature indeed,' said Sir Madoc. 'But I will face it. Never let it be said that Madoc fled quailing from any dragon, though never was one so fierce.'

'Bravely spoken,' said the king, 'and you will be just as bravely rewarded if you overcome the creature. I will give you jewels and rich treasure from my store and make you a great lord of my country.'

'My lord, you are good and generous and I will gladly chance all to defeat this dragon that spoils your golden land.' With no more words, Sir Madoc put on his armour, and took up his weapons, and rode out to challenge the dragon.

As Sir Madoc rode out into the wild country where the dragon lived, he moved with great care, keeping a constant watch for any beasts. Every tree or bush, every turning in the track, could be the hiding place for some fierce thing that could attack him so suddenly that he would have no chance to use sword or spear, before being torn from his saddle, and ripped to bleeding shreds of flesh. He watched the air too for flying foes and when he passed a lake he scanned its surface for any threatening ripple. Nothing stirred to come against him and he rode more and more deeply into the wild. The sun rose, and Sir Madoc was hot in his heavy armour, and weary of searching with never a moment when it was safe to rest. Then, on a hillside, he saw the dragon. It was in its own shape after all! It was the dragon of all the legends and pictures, with glittering scales, forked tail, staring eyes and gaping mouth full of sharp teeth, each the size of a man. It was eating something, some ragged mass of flesh that it held in its great claws, ripping and tearing at it, and sucking the blood that oozed from it. Sir Madoc shuddered but held his sword and lance ready to charge. When the dragon saw him it roared, and stamped and tore at the ground, sending a shower of grass and earth high into the air. Then it charged straight at Sir Madoc. Never wavering, Sir Madoc spurred his horse and charged straight at the dragon, holding his sharp lance. The lance firmly pointed at the softest spot any dragon has – its eyes! The two thundered towards each other. Which would be first to waver? A look of fear came into the dragon's eyes as it saw the cruel point of the lance, directed firmly at its tender eyeballs. On Sir Madoc drove; on, on, to drive his point into the dragon's left eye, and plunge it deep into the monster's brain, and so kill it at a blow. Never before had the dragon met a knight brave enough to carry this move through. Now, it wavered for a fatal second. With a cry of triumph, Sir Madoc lunged forward with all his might, to give the dragon its death blow.... There was a blinding flash of light, at the very instant when the lance was about to pierce the dragon's eye, and the dragon was gone! Sir Madoc was going so fast that he galloped on some way before he could stop. Then he reined his horse in and looked about him in great bewilderment. The dragon was nowhere to be seen. It had disappeared. Sir Madoc smiled grimly.

'Ah, I see your game, sir dragon. You have escaped death by making one of your famous changes in the nick of time. You coward! Where are you? Come out and fight fairly! Come, sir dragon, where are you now?'

Just in time, Sir Madoc thought to look upwards. A great eagle was in the act of diving on him. Quickly, Madoc fitted a shaft to his bow, aimed, and loosed it at the eagle's chest. The arrow rose to meet the eagle. Snap! The eagle disappeared, and the arrow fell harmlessly back to earth. Madoc spoke grimly: 'Do your worst, foul beast, I'm ready for you. Come on then, what is it to be next ?'

There was silence. Madoc looked all about him. He watched the trees and bushes; nothing moved. He watched the sky; only a lark rose singing above him. He watched the ground beneath his feet; only a worm dug its hole. Then, just as Madoc loosed his grip upon his sword, and breathed freely again, the grass parted near his horse's foot, as though it had been combed! It was a snake! A snake as thick as a man's body. Black and yellow, it was, in a diamond pattern, and Madoc knew at once that it was deadly poisonous. Swiftly, the snake lashed through the grass, then arched its body, ready to strike. Quickly as the snake moved, Madoc moved more quickly; he swung his great mace, with its cruel spikes of metal glistening in the sun, he swung it down, crashing upon the snake's ugly head at the very moment its fangs opened to bite. There was a heart-stopping scream and the snake vanished. The mace swished through empty air. Madoc smiled.

'Good, sir dragon, you must try harder than that,' he said. 'I nearly had you that time. Come, now, give Madoc a good battle. Come on, dragon; come out and fight, like a true dragon. Let's have an end to this nonsense!'

All was still and quiet. Madoc sat, watchful, upon his horse. Nothing moved. Madoc gazed above and about and below him. Still, nothing moved. A weary time did Madoc sit there, getting very hot and tired. He was thinking the dragon had run away and given up the fight. 'Shall we turn for home, good creature?' he asked his horse. As he bent forward to stroke the horse's neck, he noticed a tiny red spider coming down from a tree, letting itself down on its fine thread and blowing from side to side in the gentle breeze.

'What a curious little spider,' said Madoc. 'Come little creature, let me see you. Never did I see your like. Perhaps I should take you for the king's son to see. Now, if only I had a small box to put you in . . . Come little spider, I'll not hurt you.'

And he cupped his hands and held them out to catch the little red spider. Nearer and nearer, the spider came. At the very moment Madoc was going to touch the spider, a picture came into his mind. It was a picture in a book; a picture he had seen long long ago; a picture of a spider, with words printed below it. Madoc cried out, and snatched his hands away from the little red spider.

'Ah, you cunning beast!' he cried out. 'I know you, little spider. Poisonous, you are; so packed with venom that a touch means death. Dragon, I should say. How clever you are! But not clever enough to catch Madoc.'

He cut the spider's thread with his dagger and it dropped to the ground and scuttled away.

'The battle's still on, dragon,' said Madoc. 'Come on, now, and fight in your own shape, or I'll tell the world you are a coward.'

But nothing stirred. Madoc sat a long time, waiting and watching for an attack from any quarter. Nothing happened. Madoc and his horse grew weary.

'Poor beast,' said Madoc to his horse, 'you need food and water, as I do myself. Come, we'll find a place where I can stand guard while you drink your fill.'

So they went through the forest until they could hear water running quickly over stones. Madoc rode towards the sound and they came out of the trees on to the bank of a wide river. Madoc dismounted; he unharnessed the horse, and led it to the edge of the water. It drank deeply. Madoc stood upon a rock, holding his sword and lance, and looking restlessly about him for any sign of attack from the dragon. The horse drank and no attack came. It was a peaceful scene, with the river winding down the hill, and its tumbling waters flashing in the sun.

After a long time, Madoc said, 'I really do think that dragon's admitted defeat this time and gone slinking home to his cave.'

The horse stood in the river now, cooling its feet. Madoc laid down his sword and lance and took off his helmet. He knelt by the edge of the water and drank from cupped hands. He drank in the cool water and felt new life in his body. He raised his head and said, astonished, 'Whatever is that?'

A wall of water, the height of two men, was coming down the river towards them at speed. It was a great wave that foamed and bubbled and ground and tossed the stones of the river bed, with a noise like a giant grinding his teeth, and carried broken trees on its crest. Madoc only had time to cry out and hug himself to a strong tree and the wave was on them. Deep green water swirled over him and the fierce current pulled at his body, striving to drag him from his tree, to whirl him into the depths and there to drown him. But Madoc held on and the tree's deep roots held against the wave. Madoc held his breath and when he thought he could hold it no longer, the wave had passed, and his head was in air and sunshine again. Madoc gasped and sucked at the air, shook the water from him, and looked about him. The river was as calm as before. The sun glittered on its surface and began to warm Madoc's shivering body. But Madoc cried out in grief, for his horse was gone. The wave had carried it away and drowned it, brave and faithful beast that it was, and he would never see it again. Madoc's sword and lance had gone, too, and his helmet; he was defenceless, in the homeland of the dragon. He crept away from the river and fearfully made his way back. If the dragon should find him now, it could kill him and eat him without any trouble. But the dragon did not appear and Madoc reached the city safely.

Madoc was a sorry sight as he walked up to the city gates. Wet and bedraggled, without arms or helmet, he was ashamed to face the king with such a story of failure. As he came to the gates, he met an ancient man sitting in the shade of a tree. The man called to him, 'My son, what has befallen thee? Come and rest a while, and tell me thy tale. Who knows? An old man has seen many things in this world and may be able to help. Come and sit you down.'

So Madoc sat by the old man, and told him the whole story of his battle with the dragon.

'And so you see,' he ended, 'I return to your fine city a miserable failure, a beggar seeking food and rest.'

At this, the old man burst out laughing. He laughed and laughed and Madoc became angry.

'You mock me, old man,' he said. 'Foolish old man, to laugh at another's misfortune.'

'No, my son,' protested the old man. 'It is your blindness that amuses me; you cannot see what is in front of you! Look ! Look into the hills. What do you see ?'

'Only the accursed river that drowned my beloved horse. It winds like a snake, a treacherous serpent.'

'Just so, a serpent, or . . . or a dragon,' said the old man.

'A dragon? The river ? Do you mean . . . ?'

'Was that river there when you rode out this morning? Did you see it, as we do now?' asked the old man.

'No. I saw only deep forest and the mountain peaks above,' said Madoc, much amazed. 'There was no river in that place.'

'And so. . .' the old man smiled, 'your precious dragon . . .'

'Turned into a river!' cried Madoc. 'It was the river itself that it turned into at last and it tried to drown me with its great rush of waters, but took only my horse.'

'And you have defeated the dragon for all time,' said the old man.

'How so?'

'How? Did the king not tell you that the dragon was destined, one day, to take a shape that could never be changed?'

'Something of that.'

'This is the way of it. You fought it with such bravery that it turned itself into a river in despair, hoping to catch you off your guard. You could not attack a river with sword or spear, but if it had drowned you it could have become a dragon again. Now it must remain a river until the world's end and it will lash its waters in helpless fury for all time. You are the winner of the battle, not the loser. Hold your head high and enter the city in triumph. The king will heap gifts and honours upon you.'

'You put new heart into me,' said Madoc. 'And if what you say is true, you must share my good fortune. I'll take myself to the king, and tell him my story, and then see what he says. Better still, come with me and tell the king your part of the story, too. Your wisdom will help to convince him that our tale is true, for it is, indeed, a strange story we have to tell.'

So Sir Madoc and the old man walked together into the city, and came to the king's palace, and gained audience with the king. Long and earnestly they talked, and the king listened; now frowning, now amazed, now laughing. At the end of their story, the king leapt to his feet, shouting 'The foul dragon is dead forever! Rejoice, my good people, and give all honour to Lord Madoc! Rise, my noble Madoc, and take your reward. I make you a lord of my realm and you shall have wealth and lands to fit the shining honour of your brave deeds and your great name.'

Then the king arranged a great banquet to celebrate the dragon's defeat, and all over the land the people rejoiced. The king gave Madoc all that he had promised and he settled on his estates to live a good and happy life. Lord Madoc kept his promise, too, and rewarded the old man, giving him gold and a good house to comfort his old age.

The new river was, of course, named the River Dragon. No one ever went too near the River Dragon; no one ever fished in it, or swam in it, or built their houses close to it. The story of Lord Madoc's fight with the dragon was told to all the children in that country, from generation to generation, so no child was foolish enough to go near the River Dragon. To this day, it lashes its waters angrily against its banks, as though fretting to be free. If you listen carefully to the sound of its waters, you will hear a deep throated rumbling, like the growling of an imprisoned dragon. But do not go too close; it is always hoping to catch another victim, and so become a dragon again!

Two

Good medicine for a dragon

There was a town that was plagued terribly by a dragon that lived in a cave in the mountainside. It was a fierce and hungry dragon and it would rampage down the mountain, growling and spouting fire, and gobble up whatever or whoever it met; and it would go on gobbling until its enormous belly was full. At first it ate cows and sheep that it found in the high meadows. That was bad enough. Then the farmers drove their cows and sheep lower down the mountain, and kept them safely in sheds near their farmhouses. Finding no food, the dragon came farther down the mountain until he did find food. He came to the farmyards themselves and ate wandering hens and geese, pigs, donkeys and horses. The farmers packed up and fled in terror, leaving nothing for the dragon to eat. The dragon became more angry than ever, and he roared still farther down the mountain in search of his food. He came at last to the edge of the town and he was so very hungry by this time that he began to eat people! At first he snapped up a few grandmothers and grandfathers who couldn't run very fast. Then he gobbled a policeman who tried to arrest him. Then he swallowed all the crew of a fire-engine, who had gone to put out a fire he started. He munched up three teachers on their way home from school. Then, he ate a schoolyard full of children at playtime! This was too much. The town was full of terror and turmoil. Something had to be done about the dragon at once, or he would gobble everybody up.

'What we need is a dragon-slayer,' said the Mayor. 'One of those brave knights in armour who can chop a dragon's head off in a winking. That foul dragon will eat the lot of us if this goes on. He might even eat me. Quickly, now, we must offer a prize; a good prize for any brave man who can overcome that nasty greedy monster.' He sent for his scribes and messengers, and that very day the word went out to every town and city in the land, and a notice was posted on the Town Hall door itself, announcing a prize of one thousand gold pieces for any man who could save the town from its terrible dragon. This was a very good prize; enough to make a man rich for the rest of his life. Soon, knights and warriors began to arrive in the town. Some were dressed in bright armour. Some wore leather tunics. They all brought fearsome weapons; spears, cross-bows, two-handed swords, axes, forks, tridents, maces; and one even brought a small cannon, with an extra horse to pull it. The crowds cheered them on as they went, one by one, up the mountain to fight the dragon. Not one of them came back. The dragon defeated them all and gobbled them up, and licked his lips, and asked for more. He made a pile of their arms and armour outside his cave, as trophies of his battles, and the pile grew bigger and bigger. Stories of the dragon's ferocity travelled round the country and fewer and fewer knights came to do battle with him.

'Whatever shall we do?' wailed the Mayor. 'Soon there will be no one left to fight the dragon and then he'll begin to eat our people again. He'll eat our grandmothers and grandfathers; our uncles and aunts; our cousins and sisters and brothers; our mothers and fathers. He may even eat me. Oh dear, oh dear! I don't want to be gobbled up by a dragon, I don't. What can I do ?'

Then a boy came knocking at the Mayor's door one day. He was only about twelve, and he didn't look very strong, and he had no weapons or armour at all.

'What do you want?' said the Mayor.

'I've come to see about the dragon,' said the boy.

'See about the dragon?' said the Mayor. 'See about the dragon? You?'

'Yes; me,' said the boy.

'A little chap like you?'

'Yes.'

'Are you trying to be funny?'

'No. I mean it.'

'Where's your sword and armour?'

'Haven't got any.'

'Then you are trying to be funny and I'll have you whipped for it,' said the Mayor, becoming angry. 'This is no matter for jokes.'

'Truly, I'm not joking,' said the boy.

'How can a mere boy, with no weapons, kill a fierce dragon? Do you know how many brave knights have died fighting it? Dozens! And you come knocking at my door, saying you'll . . .'

'I didn't say I'd kill it.'

'What then?'

'I'll save you from it. That's what your message said. A prize of a thousand gold pieces for anyone who can save this town from the ravages of the dragon. Nothing was said about killing it. No man can kill it, I know that.'

'What then?' asked the Mayor, more puzzled than ever. 'I'll cure it. Kill or cure. If you cannot kill, you have to cure.'

'Cure it? What do you mean?'

'I'll cure it of eating people. You see, I'm a kind

of doctor for dragons. Will you give me the prize if I stop it from eating people?'

'Yes,' said the Mayor, 'but you can't do it. You'll be gobbled up like the rest of them. Still, it's worth trying, I suppose. Don't blame me if you get eaten.'

'I'd not be here to blame you, if I did,' said the boy, grinning, 'but don't worry, I'll come back to collect my prize.'

'Good luck,' said the Mayor, you'll need it. Wait a minute, I don't know your name.'

'Edward,' said the boy. 'Edward the Dragon Doctor.'

Then Edward set to work at once. He gathered a big bundle of dry sticks and grass and straw and put it in a sack. Then he went to a bakery and asked the baker to make him a big loaf of bread, the biggest he could manage, in the shape of a ball. When the loaf was ready, he painted it all over with red paint, and set it in the sun to dry. Then he took out his tinder-box, and cleaned and oiled it, and primed it with good dry tinder. Then he went off up the mountain to spy out the land and see where the dragon's cave was. He saw the dragon in the distance, but kept himself well out of sight. He noticed specially the shape of the dragon's ears, and just how they were placed on its head, and returned to the town well pleased with his afternoon's work.

There was a crowd round the red loaf of bread, but no one had touched it; as an old man had said to them, 'That's dragon medicine, I've heard tell. Don't you boys meddle with it, now.'

But when the crowd saw Edward, the cheeky boys began to jeer and make rude remarks, such as, 'Is that little shrimp going to fight our dragon? Go on, it'll gobble him up and never notice. He couldn't fight our pussycat. Come on, dragon-killer, would you like to fight me? Dare you?'

Edward took no notice of all this; even when the older men tried to persuade him not to throw his life away and a woman wept for him, saying he was so like her own boy, he only said, 'Have no fear for me; I'll be safe enough,' and, putting the red loaf in a second sack, he slung his sacks over his shoulders and went off to an inn to eat a good supper. Before he went to bed, he asked the puzzled landlord to lend him a bucket from the stables. When it was dark, and the people were asleep, Edward crept out of the inn carrying his two sacks and the bucket. He walked softly through the quiet town and away up the mountain. He filled his bucket at a spring and hid it close at hand. Then he walked straight up to the dragon's cave. No one had dared before to approach the dragon at night, but Edward was not afraid; he was sure his plan would succeed.

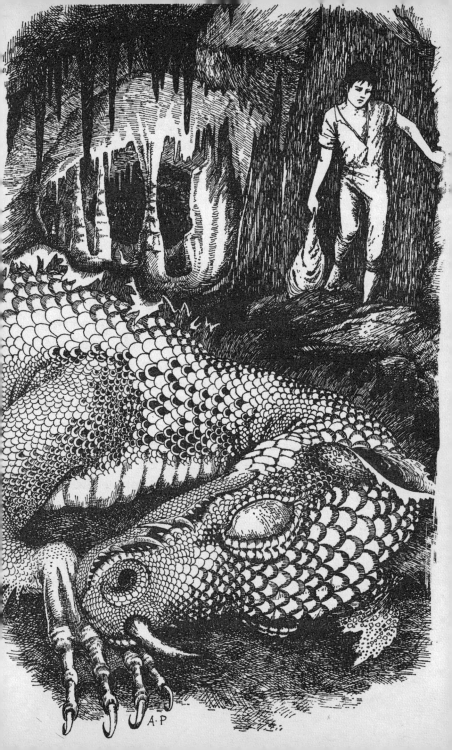

He could hear the dragon snoring and grumbling and growling in his sleep. Perhaps he was dreaming of his battles with the brave knights who had come to fight him. Edward stepped into the black mouth of the cave, feeling his way along the walls, stepping over the dragon's great claws. He climbed on to a rock just by the dragon's head. A shaft of moonlight shone into the cave. Now Edward could look down upon the dragon's fearsome face. He could see the dreadful tusks that could rip a man to shreds in a minute. He could see the glittering scales that no arrow could pierce. He could see the deep browed eyes, closed now in sleep. He could see an ear, for the dragon lay on its side; an ear, with a shaft as wide as a well, going deep into the gigantic skull. The flap of scaly skin that covered the dragon's ear had fallen back as it lay in sleep, just as Edward had hoped it would. He opened one of his sacks. He dropped the dry sticks and grass and straw right into the dragon's ear. This tickled the dragon, and it moved in its sleep, but it did not waken. Edward quickly took out his tinder-box, struck a light, and set fire to the empty sack. He let the sack blaze up, then he dropped it, too, into the dragon's ear. He scrambled off the rock, ran out of the cave, and hid behind a boulder, where he could safely see what happened. A bonfire was blazing in the dragon's ear. Clouds of smoke gushed out of it. There was a crackling as the fire reached the dry sticks and red tongues of flame licked upwards. Surely, the dragon must waken soon? There was a foul smell of scorching flesh, then the dragon screamed with pain and leaped to its feet. It came lumbering out of the cave, shaking its head frantically. It began to spout its own fire from nose and mouth, so it couldn't see that it had fire in the wrong place, too, in its ear. It screamed again and ran away up the mountain. Edward could hear it, tearing about, screaming and roaring in pain, up and down and round the mountain. The earth shook with its rampaging, and in the town the people shivered fearfully in their beds, so terrible was its noise. At last, the dragon came crawling back to its cave, whimpering with pain. Then Edward stood bravely on a rock and showed himself. When the dragon saw him, it opened its jaws wide, and came at him, to gobble him up.

'Stop,' shouted Edward. 'Don't eat me! I'm the only Dragon Doctor in the world! I'm the only one who can cure your earache !'

The dragon stopped and closed his jaws; the fire still smouldered deep in his ear and tears of pain filled his eyes.

'If I make you better, will you promise never to eat anyone again?' shouted Edward.

The dragon nodded its head vigorously up and down.

'Will you promise to live on grass and fruit and nuts?'

Again the dragon nodded.

'Then take this pill.'

Edward took the red loaf out of his sack, and tossed it into the dragon's mouth. The dragon gulped it down and a look of hope and meekness came into its eyes.

'Now close your eyes tightly, and lie down on your side,' shouted Edward. The dragon did as it was told. Edward nipped behind the rock, picked up the bucket of water, ran with it to the dragon, and tipped the water into its ear. The fire went out; the pain stopped. Edward hid his bucket.

'You can open your eyes now,' he said. The dragon gazed adoringly at Edward. Great tears of relief rolled from its eyes, and it crept forward and gently licked Edward's hand in gratitude.

'There, now, you must be a good dragon, or the earache will come back. You won't eat people, or their animals, any more, will you ?'

The dragon shook its head from side to side.

'And you promise to be good?' It nodded its enormous head.

'Then I will tell the people how to make my magical dragon's earache pills, and they'll give you one every Friday morning, and you'll never have earache. But if you become a bad dragon again, they'll stop making the pills and you will get the pain in both ears, and nothing will cure it; so remember.'

The dragon agreed to all that Edward said, and it looked sad when he said goodbye to it at last, but crept back into its cave and went to sleep.

The next day, Edward told the astonished Mayor that he had cured the dragon of eating people; and he told the baker how to make a bread pill for the dragon every Friday. He stayed a month in the town to see how the dragon behaved. His cure worked beautifully. The dragon was seen high up in the mountain, peacefully nibbling grass, and eating berries and nuts from the trees. The people lost their fear of it; Edward received his prize, and rode away in his own coach, a rich man.

The dragon never forgot Edward's medicine; there was always its Friday pill to remind it. It was a quiet and peaceful dragon after that, and as the years went by the people of the town forgot its evil days, and became quite friendly with it. They would give it pies and cakes to eat and visitors would always be taken up the mountain to see it. The town became famous as the only place in the world with a tame dragon. Tame as the dragon was, the baking of its pill, every Friday, was never forgotten. The baker taught his son to do it, and he taught his son, and so on, for many generations.

It is many long years since the old dragon died, but they still bake a dragon-loaf on Fridays, in that town; nowadays, it is not painted red, and the children eat it, with butter and jam, and no one can remember why it was first baked.

Three

The great dragon competition

This is a story that an old Grandfather Dragon used to tell to his grandchildren. His name was Quince. When the little dragons had doused their fires, and settled quietly around him, then he would begin...

"Now if you listen carefully to this story, you'll grow up to be sensible dragons, and not do foolish things, like Klart and Plodge. Who were Klart and Plodge, you say? They were a pair of dragons who came to live near here about six hundred years ago and a sillier pair you never saw. The trouble was, they were always trying to beat each other at all kinds of stupid competitions. Once, Klart said, 'I bet I can eat more trees than you, between sunrise and sunset.'

'Go on,' said Plodge. 'I'll beat you, easy.'

So they were off the next day, gobbling up acres and acres of trees, laying the countryside bare. Plodge won, but they both had a dreadful stomachache all that night, and Klart was sick, and made a mess of half-chewed trees all over the mountains. They ate nine hundred and twenty-one trees between them.

Then it was fire-breathing, and they burnt everything off the mountains for miles around, and there was nothing to eat for years and years, and a great many dragons died of starvation.

'We'll have to put a stop to their goings-on,' my dad used to say, but they were so big and strong that no one dared to try. They became sillier as they got older. Once, they had a drinking competition, and Klart drank a river dry, but he squirted it out of his mouth again, and flooded our valley, and thousands of animals and men were drowned.

'This is too much,' my dad said, but no one could stop them. Then, Grandmother Zad had an idea. She went to Klart and Plodge and said, 'There's one competition you've never had and my grandson Quince wishes to challenge you.'

'What?' they said. 'Little Quince?' And they began to laugh. I began to tremble. I thought Grandmother Zad must have grown so old (she was eight-hundred and two, at the time) that her thoughts had become muddled. How could she think of me competing with Klart and Plodge?

'Courage, little Quince,' she said, 'it is not always the biggest and strongest who win contests. Now, I'm offering a prize of a hundred gold pieces to the one amongst the three of you –

Quince, Klart and Plodge – who can fly the highest. Do you accept the challenge?'

'Yes!' shouted Klart and Plodge together.

'As for that little spark,' said Klart, looking at me, 'he won't have a chance. I can out-fly him without even trying. But Plodge, now – well, I suppose he can fly quite well, but not half as high as me.'

'Just wait ! Just wait ! I'll show you,' shouted Plodge, becoming angry. 'I'll show you how high I can fly !'

'Very well,' said Grandmother Zad. 'At dawn tomorrow, we'll all meet here for the high-flying contest.'

'But . . .' I said.

'Hush!' she said. 'Come home.'

When we were at her cave, Grandmother Zad said, 'Now, young Quince, you must follow this contest through. It is all part of a plan of mine, and I'm not going to tell anyone what it is, in case it doesn't work; but I feel sure you will win this contest. Just do your best. I don't expect you to fly higher than those two buffoons but you may win all the same. What I want you to do is to tease them, and taunt them, to make them try all the harder. You'll see. It will all work to our advantage.'

No matter how much I pleaded with her, she wouldn't tell me what her plan was, and I went home much puzzled.

The next day, a big crowd gathered on the mountain at dawn, for Grandmother Zad had passed the word amongst all the dragons about the strange contest. I thought I'd better play my part so, as soon as I saw Plodge and Klart coming, I shouted, 'Oh, look at the high-flyers! They couldn't even fly over the mountain! They haven't a chance against me! Look at their puny little wings! The sun will shrivel them if they fly as high as me.'

I went on like this for some time. The crowd of dragons began to laugh. When Plodge and Klart heard this, they began to steam and spurt fire with anger.

'The little lizard!' shouted Klart. 'How dare he compete with me? I'll take all his granny's gold, just see if I don't!'

'He's no better than a fly, that mewling Quince. Take no notice of him,' roared Plodge. 'But you're not much better yourself, old Klart. I'll leave you far behind, you'll see!'

'Oh. Oh. You boaster,' screamed Klart. 'My wings are much bigger than yours.'

'But weaker.'

They went on and on, getting furious with each other, until they were in a frenzy to begin.

'Come on, Grandmother Zad. Let's see the

prize money,' shouted Klart.

'Here it is.'

Grandmother Zad laid a big pile of gold upon the grass, and everyone gasped.

'Why all this delay? Let's get on with the contest,' said Plodge.

'Very well,' said Grandmother Zad. 'You are to fly in this order: first, Quince; second, Plodge; third, Klart. The one to fly highest and return to me, wins all the gold. My decision is final. Are you ready, Quince?'

I stretched out my wings. 'Yes,' I said, in a very small voice.

'Then - one - two - three - GO!'

I jumped into the air. My wings began to lift. I circled above the trees; up, up and up. I could see Klart and Plodge looking up and laughing at my efforts. I was higher than the top of the mountain now and still I climbed. My wings were getting tired. Oh, I must make my best possible effort, I thought, so I flapped on – up and up. Now the faces below were too small to see properly. I was very tired. 'If only I can reach the clouds,' I thought, so I struggled on with my last strength. The clouds were quite close now, just above me. One more effort! Up! And I reached them! My left wing tip swept the fringe of a feathery cloud, but now I was exhausted. I allowed my whole body to go limp. I fell through the air. I dropped. I lay on the air, as though I were on a soft bed of moss; it was a pleasant feeling for one as tired as I was. I almost forgot that I was really falling, down down down, at great speed towards the sharp rocks and the upturned faces below. Just in time, I came to myself; I opened my wings; they caught on the rushing air, with a great wrench that almost pulled them out of their sockets. I glided down in a wide circle and landed on the grass.

'Well done, my grandson,' said Grandmother Zad. 'I saw you in my telescope. You touched a cloud. A very good effort.'

Klart and Plodge sneered at this, and Klart said, 'That was nothing. Wait till you see me.'

'You wait your turn,' said Plodge. 'I'm next.'

'Yes. Are you ready?' said Grandmother Zad. 'One - two - three - GO!'

Plodge swept into the air, with a clapping of his enormous wings that nearly blew us all over. Up he went, with a swift strength that was truly astonishing. He was at the clouds in a few minutes. Then he was through the clouds and still going at speed. He seemed to become smaller and smaller as he climbed, until he was only a dot in the sky, and then not even a dot. Grandmother Zad still watched through her telescope.

'He's still climbing,' she said, 'and I do believe

he's going faster. Yes. Yes, he is increasing his speed. On he goes. Goodness, what a speed! Never in my life did I see a dragon fly so fast. Never.'

All this time, Klart was fairly dancing with impatience to be off and growling with envy at Plodge's performance, 'Just wait. I'll show you. I'll show you. I can fly higher than him. I'll fly round the sun. I'll fly round the stars . . .'

'Oh!' gasped Grandmother Zad.

'What's happened?' said Klart.

'Something's happened to Plodge. I do believe he's gone into orbit round the earth. You know, like those space-things the humans send up. He's not flapping his wings now, but he's all bundled up in a helpless sort of way, and he's going faster than ever. I do believe he's going to set.'

'*Set*?' I said, amazed.

'Not like a jelly,' she said. 'No. Like the sun; it sets and rises, and Plodge is going to set and rise, for ever and ever, I believe. There he goes! Yes, he has set.'

She laid her telescope down.

'It will be some time before he rises,' she said. 'We can go home for some dinner.'

'What about my turn?' demanded Klart.

'You must wait until we see if Plodge *is* coming back,' she said. 'Let's give him three times round the world, and if he doesn't come down then, we'll count him out of the race. I'll keep watch.'

'Oh, very well,' grumbled Klart, and everyone went home to dinner.

Grandmother Zad kept watch on the sky with her telescope, at the mouth of her cave. I kept watch while she was eating her dinner, so that I was the first to see Plodge rising, like some new moon in the sky, over the distant mountains to the South. He glowed with the reflected light of the sun and looked prettier than he had ever done on earth. He was just a ball of light, being much too far away for his head or tail to be seen. Up he came, smoothly rising in the sky. When I'd had a good look at him, I called out, 'Grandmother Zad! Plodge has risen. Come and see!'

She came at once and chuckled merrily as she gazed through the telescope.

'We'll have no more trouble from Plodge, I'm thinking. Indeed, he'll be more useful up there than he ever was on earth. We'll be able to navigate by him on night flights.'

Plodge passed across the sky and set below the horizon about supper-time.

'Now, I think he'll rise again about breakfast time,' said Grandmother Zad. 'So go and tell Klart we'll meet then for the next part of the contest.'

This, I did, and Klart roared with delight, fit to burst the mountain.

'So old Plodge really is out of the contest, this time. That leaves the field clear for me to win, and collect the gold. Ho! Ho! Wait till you see me fly, little flea. Just wait!'

The next morning we all met as before. Soon after the sun was up, Plodge rose again in the sky.

'There he goes,' cried Grandmother Zad. 'He will never come down now. I declare him out of the competition. Now it is your turn, Klart. Are you ready?'

'Ready?' said Klart. 'Ready? I've been ready since yesterday.'

'Very well. One . . . two . . . three . . .and Go!' shouted Grandmother Zad.

Klart was gone in a flurry of wings. He made such a wind that several of the smaller dragons fell over. He was already high above us, and going very fast; faster, even, than Plodge had gone. Past the mountain-tops; past the clouds; on up into the sky, he went. Now he was a dot. Now he was gone. But Grandmother Zad held him in her telescope for a time yet.

'He goes faster, still,' she said. 'I believe he's going to join Plodge in orbit. Oh, surely not? No, he's going too fast for that.'

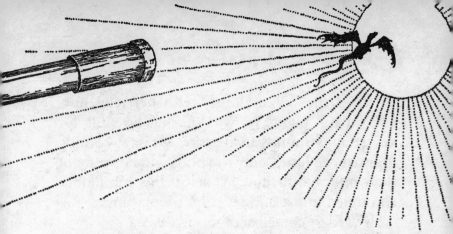

'He boasted that he would fly round the sun,' I said.

'I believe he will, too,' said she. 'He's going fast enough, and heading straight for the sun.' She took her eye away from the telescope. 'I can see no more,' she said. 'I fear the sun's glare will blind me. I must look no more.'

'Is the contest over?' everyone shouted.

'No,' she said, 'we must await his return. It will take him a whole year to go round the sun, and, who knows, he may return to claim my gold as his prize.'

So everyone went home.

Summer passed, then autumn, and winter. Many had forgotten the contest and went on with their lives – hunting for food, bringing their children into the world and digging new caves. The mountains were peaceful again without the troublesome goings-on of Plodge and Klart to disturb them. The dragons who lived in them were happy. But Grandmother Zad often searched the sky anxiously with her telescope, and on still nights we would stand listening for any strange sounds in the sky. We saw nothing unusual; we heard only the birds and creatures of the world. No shadow fell across the sun. Plodge continued to rise and set at his proper times.

'*Will* Klart come back?' I often asked.

'I cannot tell,' said Grandmother Zad. 'I cannot tell.'

Spring came, and summer again. It was now a year, and more, since Klart had flown off towards the sun. Still all was peaceful and nothing strange came out of the sky. Then, in the heart of a moonless night, we were brought tumbling out of our beds, all trembling and jelly-kneed with fear, for some great roaring sound had wakened us, and a tremendous thump had shaken the mountain ash and still the ground was shaking under us. Was it an earthquake? Had some enemy attacked us? We could not tell. We tumbled to the mouths of our caves. We looked about us.

'Look! There!' cried Grandmother Zad, pointing to the biggest mountain. Its top was gaping open and red fire gushed out of it.

'A volcano! That mountain's a volcano! That's what woke us up, and if it begins to pour out molten lava we'll all have to fly for our lives, and we'll never be able to live in this lovely valley again.'

'Did you see him?' came a crusty voice out of the darkness.

'Did I see whom? Who are you talking about? Is that you, Garboil?' said Grandmother Zad.

'Yes, it is me, and I do believe you were asleep, and didn't see him,' answered old Garboil, a dragon who often went for night walks.

'*Who?* For goodness sake make sense of yourself,' snapped Grandmother Zad.

'Well, that foolish Klart, of course,' said Garboil, laughing. 'That silly fellow who said he would fly round the sun. He came flashing out of the sky, he did, too fast to stop, all lit up with his terrible speed, all glowing, like a comet, he was, and he hit that mountain a fair wallop, he did. I've never seen anything like it in all my nine hundred years on this earth.'

'You mean, Klart did *that?*' said Grandmother Zad, pointing at the volcano.

'Course he did,' said Garboil. 'He went straight in, he did, he never even slowed down, he went straight into the mountain top. You could hear the rocks melting and hissing. Down, he went, down and down, right deep into the hot part of the earth. I don't know if he's stopped yet. Maybe he'll go right through the world and come out in Australia. I have a cousin lives there;

what a surprise he'd get! Oh, dear, what a bang he made. It was a terrible noise. He'll have wakened all the children.'

He had indeed. He had wakened everyone. Soon, a crowd gathered, and the word went round that Klart had returned from his journey round the sun, and become a volcano.

'He's the only dragon in all history who made himself into a volcano,' said Grandmother Zad. 'Poor old Klart, he really did fly too high this time. Now that he's a volcano he cannot win the prize for the competition was for dragons. I therefore award my hoard of gold to my dear grandson, Quince.'

Everyone cheered, and I blushed deeply, and Grandmother Zad told me afterwards that she'd meant me to have the gold all along, as it was no use to her, now that she was too old to enjoy it. Plodge stayed in his orbit; you can see him to this day, with a good telescope.

The volcano is still there, too, and it was named Klart, after the dragon who made it. It spurts fire now and then, and makes a nasty smell of sulphur sometimes, but it's never done worse than that. So our valley has been a peaceful place ever since.

Now, you young dragons, remember the story of Klart and Plodge, and never try to over-reach yourselves. If anyone bets you, or dares you. . .''

But the little dragons had scampered away, to play rolypoly down the mountain-side, leaving old Quince to smoke his pipe and smile over stories and memories of long long ago.

Four

The Rottingdean dragon

Rottingdean is by the sea, not far from Brighton. It is a busy place now but in the old days it was a quiet farming village, among the peaceful green slopes of the Sussex Downs. Great herds of sheep roamed the gentle hills with their shepherds watching over them. So life went on in its tranquil rural way, with the occasional excitement of a foxhunt, or a ship-wreck along the rocky coast. Rottingdean drowsed through the hot days of summer, thoroughly contented with itself; smug and snug, with its rich harvest of wool all about it. Then, something happened to make all Rottingdean shake itself wide awake.

Tom Lavender was the first to see it. He was at sea in his little boat, pulling his lobster pots in, perhaps a mile offshore from Rottingdean. It was a hot and hazy day and Tom thought at first he was seeing some sort of mirage; perhaps some boat over the horizon, reflected by a shimmering layer of hot air, and so seeming to be in the sky. There was a long grey shape, wavering up and down just above the sea, just where sea and sky met, far away towards France. Tom looked down into his boat to tip a lobster out of a pot, bait the pot, and drop it overboard. Then he looked up at the sky again. The shape was still there. It was bigger. Surely it was? Tom sat down and went on watching. It was coming nearer. It was growing bigger, much bigger. Still Tom sat and watched. Now he could see that it was some kind of bird; its wings were beating up and down in long sweeps. And yet it was more like a bat than a bird; but no bat could be that size. Tom sat a long time watching, and all the time the thing's size grew and grew as it came across the wave-tops, beating directly towards him. It is difficult, at sea, to guess the size of distant things. As the thing flew on, Tom saw that he was quite wrong.

'That's no bird,' he said. 'Not that size. It's bigger than a haystack, that is. Whatever is it ?'

Then he seized his oars and began to row for the shore. The thing was so near now that its great shadow blackened the sea and the beating of its wings raised an evil wind.

'It was bigger than ten elephants. It was bigger than twenty haystacks. It was so big it blacked the sun out.' These were some of the ways Tom told the crowd about it in the village that night. Nothing he could say would make it sound as bad as it really was, as he strained at the oars, his whole body trembling with terror. The monster's long scrawny neck stuck out in front, and as it flew it turned its fearsome head from side to side, as though looking for something. Tom had no chance of escaping. It could pluck him from the sea and swallow Tom, boat, lobsters and all, in a moment.

Luckily for Tom, it was more interested in something ahead of it, and it went flapping thunderously on towards the shore.

As it happened, no one in Rottingdean was looking out to sea at that moment. The only thing most people knew was that a black shadow had passed across the sun. But when Tom reached the shore at last, and ran shaky-legged into the village, what a hubbub greeted him! Farmers and their wives wailing, 'We're ruined! We're ruined! A lifetime's work come to naught!'

Shepherds in tears, crying, 'My flock! My poor flock!'

Crowds thronging into church to pray for deliverance, and banging on the parson's door to ask what it all meant. The whole village going mad with fear. And Tom ran up to man after man crying, 'What's happened? Tell me, what *has* happened here?'

But no one was calm enough to stop and tell him. He got no sense out of anyone until he came on Jim Henty, sitting with a long face, by

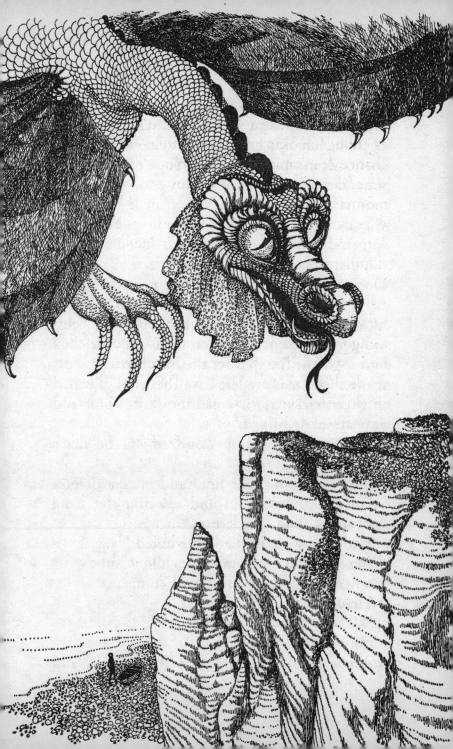

the village pond. He knew Jim well; they'd often herded sheep and worked at the shearing together. Jim was head shepherd now, at one of Rottingdean's biggest farms. Tom called out to him: 'Jim, old friend, have you enough sense in your head to tell me what's happened? Not a soul will talk to me; not to mean anything. What is it Jim? And why are you looking so down?'

'Why, you must have been at sea,' said Jim. 'Don't you know? Half our sheep are gone, and the Downs are burning. They say it was a dragon out of France. It fell upon the sheep in the fields and gobbled them by the score. Then it belched a great gob of fire that set the hills blazing. Most of the sheep that are left have the wool scorched on their backs. It's a dreadful affair, Tom, and we're all surely ruined.'

'A dragon?' said Tom wonderingly. 'So that's what it was.'

'Aye, a dragon,' said Jim, 'and once a dragon strikes, it strikes again and again at the same place, until all is a wilderness.'

'But it took no people?' Tom asked.

'No. No man, or woman, or child is hurt.'

'Then we have a chance,' said Tom.

'How so?'

'We must fight it!'

'You're a fool to say so.'

'*You're* a fool to say no,' said Tom angrily, 'and

if we weren't old friends I'd not forgive you for it. We must stand firm, don't you see, Jim?'

'No, it's no use,' said Jim, heavily. 'Folks are packing up already. There's nothing to do but run away from such a dreadful thing.'

'Nonsense,' shouted Tom. 'I love Rottingdean and I'll never leave it. No rotten old dragon's going to make me run away. We must fight it.'

By now, a crowd had gathered round them, listening to the argument.

Someone shouted, '*How* can we fight a dragon ?'

'Yes, how? How?' the shout was taken up.

'I'll show you how,' said Tom. 'Yes, I'll show you. Give me the help of ten strong men and I promise to rid Rottingdean of the dragon.'

'You're a brave man, Tom,' said Jack Lovett, the parson, 'and I'll be the first to help in any scheme you have. I'll find nine more good strong men, too, to join us before sundown.'

'Thank you, parson,' said Tom, and he went off to his cottage, to think out a plan of campaign for, in truth, he had no idea at that moment just how such an enormous dragon could be fought.

Tom sat up half the night, thinking out a plan. By dawn, he had a daring idea. He whispered it to the parson but it was a close secret between them. Immediately after breakfast, parson Lovett called out his nine good men, and they all went off along the cliff-path to Brighton, with Tom Lavender leading.

Not to be outdone, Jim Henty went down to the beach with a dozen other men, all carrying bows and arrows. All morning, they kept watch, out to sea.

'I know where Tom's gone,' said Jim. 'He's gone to see the Captain at Brighton Battery, to ask him to bring his cannons to Rottingdean, to kill the dragon. But they'll not come. It's as much as their lives are worth. I know, my brother's in the regiment. Their orders are to defend Brighton and they stay at their post whatever happens. They fear the French more than they fear any dragon.'

Jim was only partly right, as we shall see. Tom *had* gone to see the Captain at the Battery, where the big guns pointed always towards France, but not to ask for cannons.

About noon, the dragon came again. It came low over the sea, out of the shimmering heat-haze. Jim and his men stood their ground. They strung their bows, and took careful aim. The fearful bulk of the dragon filled their sky.

'Wait, now!' called Jim. 'Fire!'

They aimed at the dragon's belly. Thirteen arrows rose into the air. Thirteen arrows struck the dragon's belly. Thirteen arrows bounced back, and fell clattering on the stony beach, all amongst the dismayed bowmen. The dragon took no notice; it flew on towards the Downs, quite untroubled.

All this time, Tom Lavender and his men were struggling and sweating and cursing, as they staggered back along the path from Brighton, for each man carried a cannon-ball! Even Jack Lovett, the parson, carried one, and he cursed best of them all, for his curses were holy ones that had all the thunder of the Old Testament in them. At the Battery, Tom had told the Captain about the dragon.

'The cannons stay here,' the Captain had said, as Tom expected. So he told him his secret plan. The Captain had roared with laughter, shouting, 'You'll never do it! What a joke! Well, but you're plucky. I'll give you a bag of powder, and you can take a ball each. So much I'll do for you, if you carry the balls yourselves. The parson, too! Ho! Ho! What a sight!'

At first, the men had refused to carry the cannon-balls, when they felt their weight.

'You must be off your head,' grumbled Adam Follett. 'What's the use of cannon-balls without a cannon to fire them?'

So Tom had to tell them all his desperate plan

and they began to smile, then to laugh, and soon each man heaved a cannon-ball into his arms, and they began the painful walk to Rottingdean, a struggling line of men, splay-footed and bow-legged under the strain. Tom carried, too, a sack of gunpowder.

That was a walk that each man remembered the rest of his days. The terrible weight of the cannon-balls dragged at their arms and legs, making every muscle ache. Time and again, they stopped to rest. Each time, Tom thought they would leave the cannon-balls where they lay and refuse to carry them another inch. Each time, he encouraged them with talk of the dragon and the terrible things it would do if they did not kill it. In spite of all he said, some were ready to stop.

'This is too much for mortal men,' growled Adam Follett. 'I say we're a load of fools.' Just then they all saw the dragon coming over the sea. Without another word, each man hoisted his burden, and groaned onward.

It was dusk when Tom and his men came toppling into Rottingdean. Once again, the village was full of moaning and weeping. The dragon had brought greater destruction. It had eaten fifty sheep. It had set fire to Bill Parslow's barn and Granny Wilkinson's cottage was burnt to the ground. People were wild with fear, and more families were packing all their belongings on to carts, ready to flee.

People stood amazed at the sight of the group of weary men, almost on their knees and weeping with exhaustion, as they came into the village. Strong men rushed to help them and the women brought beer and cheese to refresh them. On Tom's instructions the cannon-balls were taken to a row of houses that faced the sea, and had a good view of it.

The next morning, there was great activity in and out of those houses. Hammerings, and clinkings, and bangings, came from them. Much mortar was mixed in the gardens, and loads of stone and bricks carried in. Men sat on roofs, and shouted down the chimneys, giving instructions to the men who worked inside. Tom was here and there, giving instructions, inspecting the work. Now and then, he gazed out to sea, watching for the dragon, but no dragon came all that day, and the work was finished to Tom's satisfaction by nightfall.

'Do you think it will work?' he said to Jack Lovett.

'We can only pray that it will, now,' said the parson. 'We have done all that is humanly possible to save our village. Let us await the morning with good faith.'

They went to bed full of hope. The rest of the village, Tom's helpers apart, were full of wonder and puzzlement, for Tom's secret had been kept. Whatever was Tom up to? They must sleep that night in ignorance, for none could ever guess.

The next day dawned clear. Tom was up early, watching the sea. Jack Lovett was quickly at his side and the others went to their posts. A man was posted at each of the eleven houses in the row at which all the previous day's work had been done. There was no sign of the cannon-balls, or the gunpowder. Crowds of people came to watch but they saw nothing. The morning passed quietly. Tom watched. The dragon did not come. The sun reached its height. A light breeze sprang up. The church clock chimed the hours; two o'clock, three o'clock; and still no dragon.

'What's happening? Is the dragon coming? What's Tom Lavender and parson up to?' The people questioned each other anxiously, but no one had any answers.

Four o'clock. Still no dragon.

'I fear he's not coming today,' said Jack Lovett.

Just then, Tom saw a faint shadow far out to sea. 'Wait,' he said. 'Wait. There's time, yet.'

The shadow moved; it grew; it was the dragon!

'He's coming,' whispered Tom. 'Look! He's

coming, at last. Is all ready?'

'Yes. Everything.'

'Wait for my order. Warn the men.'

As before, the dragon grew in size as it came on. The men watched, tense with excitement. The dragon drove steadily on, aimed directly at Rottingdean, its wings beating steadily, up and down, up and down. Nearer. Now they could see its jaws, its blazing eyes. Now it was over the beach. Now over the first houses of the village, its shadow reaching out towards Tom. Tom waited. His men waited inside the row of houses. When the dragon was directly overhead, Tom shouted,

'F I R E!'

Each of the eleven chimneys suddenly spurted smoke and fire; each spat a cannon-ball into the air. There were eleven sickening thumps as the balls hit the dragon and buried themselves in its flesh. The dragon screamed and flung itself about in the air. The speed of its motion carried it beyond the village, although its wings were in tatters. It slumped into the hillside, a mixed mass of torn flesh, with gouts of blood spurting from it, and stinking fire reeking on its dying breath.

Tom's men came out of the houses looking dazed.

'Did it work?' they said.

'Look,' said Tom, pointing at the hill.

Tom shook hands with them all.

'We've done it,' they said. 'We've done it.'

Soon, all the village was out on the hill, looking at the terrible ruin of the dragon. The word went round, how Tom Lavender had used chimneys as cannons, bricking up the fireplaces below; with a charge of gunpowder and a cannon-ball inside; and Tom was a hero in those parts for the rest of his life. People came from all over the country to see the dead dragon. The villagers quickly built a fence round the dragon and charged five shillings to see it. The money was shared among the villagers, and they soon had enough to buy new flocks of sheep to replace the ones the dragon had eaten.

Peace and prosperity returned to Rottingdean, thanks to Tom Lavender and his famous Rottingdean cannons.

Five

A race with a dragon

There was once a brave knight who went out to fight a dragon. He had killed so many dragons in his time that there was no fear in his heart as he rode out upon the mountain-side to meet the beast. He would finish it off, he thought, and be home in time for dinner. But he was wrong. The dragon was stronger and more ferocious than any he had met before. The battle raged about the mountain all day. Again and again, the knight thrust at the dragon's body with spear and sword. Each time, the dragon's scales turned the blade aside. It seemed to have no weak spot. Again and again, the dragon roared and charged the knight. The knight's horse wheeled and twisted, dodging away at the last moment from the dragon's snapping jaws. Horse and rider grew weary, and as night came on, it seemed as though the dragon must win the battle. The knight's horse stumbled and the knight fell heavily to the ground. The dragon stood over him, and opened its jaws wide, to crunch him up; but the knight called out to the dragon, 'Stop, foul beast! You must not eat me yet! It is written in the Rules of Dragon Combat that you must give me a fair chance. My horse and weapons are gone. I cannot fight you. The Dragon Lord himself will punish you, if you eat me now.'

The dragon stopped, its mouth still open. The knight's words troubled it and it stepped back a pace. It knew well enough that the Dragon Lord's word had stood as a pact between dragons and men for a thousand years past, but it was hungry, and had hoped to snap up this morsel without argument.

'Oh,' it said. 'So you know about that do you?'

'Yes, I do,' said the knight, 'and I claim my right to fair combat.'

'But the rules say, if I remember well,' said the dragon, wickedly, 'that I can make the terms, as you are at my mercy.'

'Yes,' said the knight. 'That is true. Make your terms, sir dragon; I will keep them.'

'Very well,' said the dragon, 'we will have a race.'

'A race?' said the knight, going pale.

'A race,' said the dragon. 'If I win, I may eat you. If you win, you may go free. And the course is once round the world, and back here, beginning at dawn tomorrow.'

'What chance is there for me?' said the knight, gazing at the powerful legs and the great folded wings of the dragon. Then, as he looked at the dragon's bony spine, and its long flat tail, he cheered up, and said, 'I accept your terms, dragon. I'll meet you at dawn.'

'You'd better,' said the dragon. 'If you don't come, I'll ravage the town that hides you. I'll burn all the houses to the ground, and kill every man, woman and child in them.'

'A knight always keeps his word. I'll be there.'

The knight went off among the trees, calling for his horse. The dragon went back to its lair, well pleased with itself.

Next morning, the knight was out before dawn, and waiting on the mountain for the dragon. As the sun rose, the dragon came yawning out of its cave.

'Is it you, knight?' it said. For the knight had taken his armour off, for lightness and speed, so looked quite different.

'Yes,' said the knight, 'I am the one who fought with you yesterday, and I am here now to race you once round the world, as promised.'

'Are you ready, then,' said the dragon. 'When I count three . . .'

'Just a moment,' said the knight. 'How are we to line up for the start? You are a good forty feet long, so if I stand nose to nose with you, then you are giving me a forty-foot start, and that isn't fair to you.'

'Pooh, I don't care,' said the dragon. 'What's a mere forty feet when we're going all the way round the world? You haven't a chance of winning, anyway. You can have your forty feet.'

'Oh, no, I insist on absolute fairness,' said the knight, 'then there can be no argument about the result. I don't want to have to fight you again and I can run faster than you think.'

'Oh, very well,' said the dragon. 'Have it your own way. Go and stand by my tail, and let's be off.'

'One more thing,' said the knight.

'What *now*?'

'If I win, you must also promise not to eat people any more, or burn houses down, or trouble the people in any way. Then I will be able to collect half the reward I would have had for killing you.'

'Certainly. Certainly,' said the dragon. 'You'll not live to collect any reward, so it doesn't matter what I promise. Now, are you ready to begin?'

'Yes,' said the knight, taking his place by the dragon's tail.

'I cannot see you, are you there, by my tail?'

'Yes, I am here,' answered the knight.

'One, two . . . GO!' roared the dragon.

At 'two' the knight jumped on to the dragon's flat tail, and held tightly on to its bony knobbles. Off went the dragon, galloping across the countryside. The speed of its going made a great wind that whooshed across its back, and nearly blew the knight from his perch, but he held on with all his strength. The vast tail also swayed up and down as the dragon lolloped along, and it was like riding on some enormous switchback, a nightmare ride over fields and forests, high mountains and wide plains. When they came to a river, the dragon simply jumped across. When they came to the Irish Sea, the dragon spread his wings and flew. Now the ride was smoother and the knight could rest a little. When it landed in Ireland, the dragon paused for breath.

'How are you doing, knight?' it said. 'Are you keeping up with me?' And it looked round to see where he was. Quickly, he jumped off the tail, and sat down on the grass.

'Here I am!' he shouted. 'I'll just rest while you rest, though I'm not even puffed, as you are. I told you I could run faster than you think.'

'But how did you cross the sea?' asked the amazed dragon.

'I swam underwater, like a fish. I was way ahead of you.'

'I'll show you,' said the dragon. 'I can go much faster than that. I was only warming up then. Now we'll *really* race.'

Luckily for the knight, this dragon was of a breed not noted for intelligence, and its hide was

so thick that it felt nothing as he jumped upon its tail again, just in time, too.

Faster and faster they went and crossed Ireland in a few minutes. Now they faced the wide Atlantic Ocean, but the dragon spread its wings without pausing, and soared high into the sky. Thousands of miles of glittering ocean slipped by

below them and still the dragon flew tirelessly on. They reached Newfoundland by eleven o'clock but the dragon didn't land. He went on until the Great Lakes came into view, then he made a long gliding descent, and landed on the shores of Lake Ontario. There he had a long, long drink. Then he looked about him.

'Are you there, knight?' he said, grinning nastily. 'No, I've left him well behind now. I'll have a good long rest by this cool lake.'

'Oh no you won't,' said the knight. 'I'm still with you. The race is a draw, so far, sir dragon!'

The dragon groaned and grumbled, but he got to his feet. He seemed a little tired, now. The knight jumped on his tail again and off they went. Across America they galloped – through Ohio, Indiana, Illinois, Missouri and Kansas. They rested near Dodge City, then on through Colorado, Utah and Nevada. At last they came to California and paused by the vast Pacific Ocean. The dragon spread his wings again and flew out towards the horizon. They landed in Japan at tea-time and the dragon was surprised to find that the knight was still with him. Off across China, they went, then north into Russia. Darkness was coming on now, and as they galloped along they saw the lights of villages, towns and cities, gleaming in the blackness. Oh, how they both longed to stop for food and rest.

But there is no stopping in such a race, so on and on they went.

'Are you still there?' asked the dragon, as they passed the Caspian Sea.

'Yes!' called the knight, in the dark.

They crossed Poland, Germany, Belgium, and at last they stood by the English Channel, and looked across to England and home.

The dragon barely had the energy to fly across the Channel, and landed on Dover beach, with almost all his strength gone. Slowly, he crawled up the length of England, and came at last to his own mountain. He lay down, and rolled over, panting, on to his back. The knight jumped off just in time to escape being squashed.

'Are you there?' gasped the dragon.

'Yes, I'm here,' said the knight, 'and I'm not even out of breath.'

'You're a great racer,' said the dragon, 'but you haven't won. It was a draw.'

'Agreed,' said the knight. 'So what's to be done? I haven't lost, so you cannot eat me.'

'And I haven't lost, so you cannot keep me to all my promises,' the dragon replied.

'I'll tell you what I'll do,' said the knight. 'If you *will* keep your promise not to trouble the people, then I can collect the reward and I will share it with you. Five hundred gold pieces for you, and five hundred for me. What could be fairer than that?'

'Oh, I'm too tired to argue,' groaned the dragon. 'Never again will I challenge anyone to a race round the world. I had no idea it was so far. Still, it would be nice to have five hundred gold pieces. The best dragons always had a hoard of gold and I've never had any. Yes, I agree, knight. Go and collect the gold and I swear to keep all my promises.'

So the knight went and told his story to the mayor of the town, and the mayor gave him the half-reward of one thousand gold pieces, and the knight shared it with the dragon. The dragon loved the shiny golden coins, and spent many a dark winter day counting them and playing with them. As for the knight, he had enough money to keep him in comfort for the rest of his days, so he retired from knighthood, and lived peacefully, growing apples and keeping pigs; never again did he need to face death for reward, on the field of battle, or in combat with dragons and monsters.

If anyone said, 'Wouldn't you like to travel and see the world in your old age?' he would say, 'I've seen enough travelling to last me all my life. After all, I have been round the world.' But he always kept it a secret, how he had been round the world. He didn't dare to think what would happen if the dragon discovered how he had been tricked!

Six

The man who asked questions and how he met a dragon

In Ancient Greece there was once a man called Apollonius. He lived in a village in the mountains and he was famous in that part of the country for his jokes and his questions. His jokes would set any gathering roaring with merriment; but his questions puzzled everyone, most of all himself. He would ask things such as, 'Why doesn't the sea fall off the edges of the world?' Or, 'What holds the sky up?' Or, 'What is the smallest thing possible in all creation?' Or, simply, 'What is there beyond?'

People became angry, when they heard all these questions.

'Why does Apollonius ask such silly questions?' they would say. 'They're bothersome things to think about, unsettling, they are. Isn't life hard enough, getting enough to eat, and keeping the wolves from the goats, without asking questions that cannot be answered? The sky hasn't fallen down yet, so who cares what holds it up? Apollonius should see to his olives and never mind the sky.'

But Apollonius took no notice. He went on asking questions, and the older he grew, the more troublesome his questions became. When people grew too angry with him, he would tell them jokes to cheer them up.

One day, Apollonius was plying his aged grandfather, Mindarus, with questions, in his usual way. After a stream of questions that even the oldest and wisest man could not answer, Mindarus lost all patience, and snappishly said, 'Get you gone to Delphi, you troublesome fellow!'

'To Delphi, grandfather?'

'Yes, to the great Temple of Apollo. Put your questions to the oracle of the great god Apollo himself; perhaps it will give you an answer that will quieten your wagging tongue.'

'But it is the greatest oracle in all the world, men say.'

'Quite so. All the world goes to Delphi with questions that can be answered nowhere else. Kings and common men go there – why not you ?'

Apollonius gazed with wonder upon his grandfather. 'I *will* go!' he cried. 'My dear, wise, Mindarus, I give you thanks. You have put great joy into my heart. I had never thought of it, that

I, Apollonius, could go to Delphi itself with my questions. Surely, golden Apollo will hear me?'

'It is said that few are turned away without an answer,' said Mindarus. 'Your questions will be no great difficulty in that holy place; but you must take golden offerings for the priestess. I am an old man. I have no use for gold. You may take what I have and good chance go with you.' And Mindarus brought a pouch of gold and silver pieces, and gave it to Apollonius, who was speechless, for once, with gratitude.

The next day, Apollonius set out for Delphi. He carried enough food for the five days of hard walking that lay before him, and a blanket for the cold nights. The whole village turned out to see him off and cheer him on his way. They were all glad to see him go.

'Now we'll have some peace,' they said, 'without his questions buzzing about our ears.'

For two days, Apollonius walked at a steady pace, resting at night in an olive grove. On the third day, he came to a wild and rocky place, where the path went along a narrow ridge. It was just wide enough for two men to pass each other, but there was a steep drop on both sides of the path, with jagged rocks far below; a strong gust of wind, or a footing lost on a loose stone, and the unwary traveller would tumble over, and be dashed to pieces. So Apollonius walked with great care. He was only a little way along this path, when he met a man coming the other way. The man was rather fat and Apollonius began to tremble at the thought of squeezing past him. When they met, the man was clearly just as frightened, and they clung to each other like old friends, and fumbled their feet together, and turned about like some queer top, to pass round each other. At last it was done, and both were still on the path, though much shaken, and they sat down to mop their faces, and calm down, and talk a little before passing on.

'Are you going to Delphi?' said the man.

'Yes,' said Apollonius.

'So am I,' said the man.

'But you're going the wrong way,' said Apollonius.

'I know,' said the man, 'but you'll not get there either the way you're going.'

'Why?' said Apollonius.

'There's a dragon guarding this path.'

'A dragon?'

'Yes, a dragon. A small dragon, but fierce, for all that. He'll only let you pass if you give him all the gold in your pouch.'

'But I must take my gold to Delphi. It's no good going on without it,' said Apollonius.

'Exactly,' said the man. 'That's why I've turned back. I'm going the long way, round the other side of Mount Parnassus. It will be twenty days walking, or more, but I'll still have my gold.'

'Twenty days,' said Apollonius. 'I cannot walk so long. My food is almost gone now and my legs are weary. Does this dragon talk?'

'Yes.'

'Then I'll talk it into letting me pass. I'm a good talker. I'll trick it somehow.'

'Oh no you won't, I tried that.'

'We'll see,' said Apollonius. 'I'll be at Delphi before you.'

'We'll see,' said the man. 'Goodbye and good luck with the dragon!'

'Goodbye and good walking!'

The two of them parted, and went on their way.

Apollonius walked on, along the narrow path, thinking hard to find a way to outwit the dragon that lay ahead of him. He had gone some way when he met another man coming the other way. This was a tall man, with a long beard.

'Good day,' said Apollonius, 'have you seen the dragon?' 'Oh, so you know about it, do you?' said the man. 'And yet you still go on towards it. Are you mad?'

'No,' said Apollonius, 'I just want to go to

Delphi, and get there quickly too, for I have little food.'

'I also am on my way to Delphi,' said the man, 'but I cannot pass the dragon; I fear I must go the long way round. I tried every trick I know with that dragon but I cannot pass it.'

'I'll tell it jokes,' said Apollonius. 'I'm good at jokes. I'll put it into such a good mood that it *will* let me pass.'

'Jokes?' said the man. 'Jokes, indeed? I've been telling it jokes all morning, and I'm famous for my jokes in Athens, but that doesn't work with this one. Yes, it laughed greatly, but still watched me closely. I tried to sneak past, and it nearly had my leg off. I tried telling it I was a magician, and that I would turn it into a frog. It didn't believe me. I tried climbing down the side of the mountain, but I almost fell over the cliff, and the dragon just sat there laughing at me. No, there's no getting past it.'

'Well, I'll have a try, if I can just get past you first!' said Apollonius.

Then they began shuffling along sideways, to squeeze past, and the man began to teeter on the edge, and seemed as if he must topple over, until Apollonius caught him by his beard and pulled him back. At last they got past each other.

'I'll wait for you here,' said the man, 'and we can walk the long way together.'

'Oh no, I'm going *this* way,' said Apollonius.
'Goodbye!'

But the man sat down to wait all the same.

Apollonius went on along the path, looking out
for the dragon. For some time he only saw rocks,
then the path went higher still, passing a
shoulder of the mountain, and next to the path
there was a small cave. Sitting in the mouth of
the cave was a dragon. It was not big, as dragons
go, only about the size of a cow; but it was quite
big enough to block the path, and to eat a man if
it so chose. It was grinning at Apollonius, with

its long blue tongue lolling out of its mouth, and showing a double row of very sharp teeth.

'Good day, dragon,' said Apollonius, cheerfully.

'Tulip,' said the dragon.

'Tulip?' said Apollonius. '*Tulip?*'

'My name,' said the dragon, showing its teeth.

'Oh,' said Apollonius, removing the smile from his face. 'I beg your pardon. Good morning, Tulip! My name's Apollonius.'

'Stop, Apollonius,' said Tulip.

'What?'

'I said stop. Where are you going?'

'To Delphi, to put a question to the oracle of Apollo.'

'Then give me your gold.'

'I cannot give you my gold; I have to take it as an offering to Apollo.'

'Then you cannot walk along my path.'

'Your path?'

'Yes.'

'Who says it's yours ?'

'I do.' With this remark, the dragon breathed out a lick of fire, that singed Apollonius's eyebrows. He took a quick step backwards.

'Oh. . . I see,' he said. 'But. . . why do you want gold?'

'Well,' said Tulip, 'it's a long story, and I'm tired of telling it. I'm thinking of having it printed in a book; but to be short, I am one of a large family, and there just wasn't enough gold to go round, and as I was the youngest I had none at all. Now every proper dragon has a hoard of gold to guard, every story about dragons says so. I want some gold. You have some. You cannot go on my path unless you pay with all the gold you have. If you want to fight you can do, then I'll eat you up and have your gold just the same. The other two turned back. Are you going to?'

'Certainly not,' said Apollonius.

'Well, then?' said Tulip.

'Well, then?' said Apollonius. 'Have you heard the joke about the man who . . .'

'*No* jokes,' said Tulip. 'I've had quite enough from the bearded one.'

'No jokes,' said Apollonius, weakly.

'You won't get round me that way, or any other way,' said Tulip. 'I'm tougher than I look.'

'Are you?'

'Yes.'

'Oh.' With this, Apollonius went back along the path, until he was a safe distance from the dragon, and sat down on a rock to think. He thought, 'This is even harder than asking questions! How am I going to get past that dragon? How? How? How? The others tried and had to turn back. Can I do it? I saw a lot of bones in his cave. I wonder if they were people who tried to fight Tulip? Come on, Apollonius, you're a clever fellow. Surely you can think of a way? Find Tulip's weakness. He must have one; everyone has a weakness; find that, and the battle's won! It's my wits against his strength. Now. . . let me think.' He sat a long time like this, talking to himself and thinking to himself, and working out plan after plan, not one of them, he could see, with any chance of succeeding. Then, at last, just as the sun was beginning to set, he noticed that the dragon had dropped off to sleep.

'Now's my chance,' he whispered. 'Why didn't I think of it before?' He began to tip-toe quietly, so very quietly, up the path towards the sleeping beast. Nearer and nearer he crept. Still Tulip slept on. Now he could almost touch its paws. Now he must step over them. Gently, he trod. Now he was past! Out of the gathering darkness, a loud voice said, 'Where do you think *you're* going?'

'Er . . . what?'

'Don't try to run for it; I can easily catch you. I'll give you "three" to step back to where you came from. If you don't, I'll eat you. One . . . two . . .'

Apollonius stepped quickly over Tulip's paws again and retreated down the path.

'In case you're thinking of trying *that* again,'

Tulip shouted after him, 'I can smell you in my sleep, so don't think that you can cheat me!' Then it settled its head on its paws, and closed its eyes again.

Now Apollonius was in despair. He could not think of any way to outwit the dragon. Yet he still refused to turn back. He unrolled his blanket, and made himself a hard bed, right in the middle of the path. He lay down and gazed at the stars in the night sky. His questions began to pick at his mind again. What was beyond all those stars? What were they made of? Could it be true that each one was a world, with men living on it? 'I must reach Delphi; I must go along the path that will lead to an answer,' he said to himself. 'But how? Ah, how?' With all these questions wandering round in his head, he fell asleep. The stars moved round the sky above him. The dragon slept, with his nose scenting every breeze. The silent moon rose. Nothing moved.

Morning came and Apollonius awoke just as the sun broke above the mountains. At that moment, an idea came to him.

'I have it,' he whispered. 'The dragon's weakness. I have found it.' He rolled his blanket up, and approached Tulip, who had also wakened.

'Well,' said Tulip, 'have you decided to give me the gold?'

'I have a better idea than that,' said Apollonius.

'I'm not listening, you'll only try to trick me. Choose: gold, go back, or be eaten. I'll not agree to anything else.'

'You'll get more gold than I have, if you will listen.'

'More? How can I?'

'All who go to Delphi must walk through a fearsome gorge to reach the Temple. It is dark and narrow and filled with thick bushes.'

'What is all this to me? Anyway, I'm not listening. Go on.'

'People come from all the world to Delphi, carrying precious gifts of gold and silver; hundreds come, every week, even kings and princes, with their servants and attendants, all carrying gifts.'

'So?'

'How many pass along *this* path?'

'Two or three each week.'

'There you are, then.'

'Where?'

'In a poor spot for collecting gold.'

'Oh. I'm not listening to you, you know.'

'Why don't you come with me to Delphi and become its guardian dragon? You'd have piles of treasure in no time.'

'Take it *all* from them?' Now the dragon's eyes gleamed with greed.

'Oh, no, Tulip! Everyone would stop coming then and you'd get no more. No, you should exact a tribute; let's say one tenth part of all their treasure. Ten gold pieces out of every hundred. One silver goblet out of every ten. That would be fair. They'd pay that in return for a safe passage through the gorge. You'd have to keep the wolves down, of course, but that would be easy for you.'

'Well . . .'

'Are you coming? I'll show you the way if you promise not to eat me, and to let me pass free, whenever I wish.'

'It sounds like a good idea,' said Tulip, slowly.

'Perhaps I will turn back, after all,' said Apollonius, pretending to do it.

'No. Come back! Don't go back!' shouted Tulip. 'I've thought about it. Yes. I have. I'll come with you. I'll try your idea.'

Apollonius smiled broadly. 'I knew you'd see sense. They say our Greek dragons are the wisest in all the world. One more thing, Tulip, my friend.'

'What's that?' asked Tulip, suspiciously.

'If I could ride on your back, we would get

there much more quickly, and the sooner you could begin collecting your gold.'

'Very well. Jump on and hold tight; I'm going to gallop.'

'Ready!'

'Oh, and *I* have one more thing to say,' said Tulip, turning his head to look up at Apollonius.

'Yes, my dear Tulip?'

'If this is a trick; if you are thinking of cheating me, watch out! I could gobble you up in a winking!'

'My dear Tulip, I'd not dream of tricking you,' said Apollonius. 'Come – let us be away to Delphi!' And away they galloped.

So it was that Apollonius made the most amazing entry into the city of Delphi ever known in all history, riding on a dragon! Great crowds gathered in the streets to see their passing. Children gaped. Women screamed. Strong men turned pale. All roads were open to Apollonius and Tulip; horses and carriages hurried out of their way, specially when Tulip blew out a curlicue of fire for extra effect, and they swept through the city at speed.

When they reached the gorge leading to the Temple of Apollo, they galloped through it without stopping until they reached the Temple Gates. Apollonius climbed off Tulip's back. Tulip said, 'You spoke truly of the richness of this place and its people. I will live well and contentedly here. Go on your way, and farewell!'

'Farewell, good Tulip,' answered Apollonius. 'May the gods smile on you. Goodbye!'

Tulip ran off amongst the trees, to find a comfortable cave to live in, close by the path. Apollonius entered the Temple to put his question to the oracle of the god.

Five days later, Apollonius returned to his village. He was a worn and weary man, for of course he had had to walk all the way back, having no dragon to ride upon; and walking seemed slow indeed, after his wild gallop to Delphi. When he had eaten and rested, old Mindarus, his grandfather, sat down to talk to him.

'I must ask you what all the people are asking,' he said. 'Have you brought back an answer from Delphi, an answer to all your questionings?'

'Yes, grandfather, I have, and I thank you for sending me and giving your gold for this great purpose. I had many adventures on my way and it is something I will keep with me all the days of my life.' Then he went on to tell him of his meeting with the dragon and how he won his way with it.

'But what of the answer?' said Mindarus. 'What of the answer from Delphi? May we not hear it?'

'Ah, no, my dear Mindarus, I cannot tell it to anyone. The oracle gives her answers in riddles and the answer may be more puzzling than the question. I'm still thinking about it, and I expect I will go on thinking about it for the rest of my life.'

'I cannot make head nor tail of what you're saying, my boy,' said Mindarus, shaking his head, 'but you've come back safely, at least. And now you are back, will you make our heads buzz again with more foolish questions?'

'No. I'll keep them to myself. I'll be too busy thinking about that answer,' said Apollonius, smiling.

And that is how it was. Apollonius was a quiet and thoughtful man after that. He cared for his family and tended his crops. He came to be known for his gentle wisdom, and if anyone was in trouble, or needed advice, they came to him and listened carefully to all he said, and went away the better for it. The village grew to be proud of him, and people would point him out to strangers, saying, 'Look! There goes the man who rode upon a dragon, and brought back an answer from Delphi, from the great god Apollo himself!'

Seven

Sylvia and the dragon

A long time ago, when dragons still roamed the wild parts of the earth, there was a girl called Sylvia, who lived in a land of mountains, and lakes, and deep forests. She had never seen a dragon. She lived in a quiet valley, where her father had a small farm, and kept bees at the edge of the forest. She was very happy, because she had two brothers and two sisters, and they loved each other dearly, and they worked and played together every day of the year. Her mother and father were good and kind, and there was always enough to eat, with sweet corn from the fields, and sweet honey from the bees. So they all lived peacefully for many years.

When Sylvia was seventeen, something happened to spoil all their happiness. The King came hunting in the forest on the hill above their valley. His men lost their way and came to the farm demanding food for themselves and their horses. Now this king was King Solander the Second, and, like his father before him, he was a fierce man, who loved war and plunder.

Whatever he wanted he took and no one could say no to him. Now when he came riding up to Sylvia's home, he came for food, and all the best the farm could produce was laid before him without question, even though the family would go hungry for weeks afterwards. That was bad enough, but worse was to follow, for when the King set eyes on Sylvia he fell in love with her, and wanted her for his wife. What the King wanted had to be. No amount of weeping would make any difference. And Sylvia did weep, most piteously, for she had no wish to be wife to a king, and live in a cold stone castle far away from her beloved family. The King already had thirteen wives, for in that country it was the custom for noblemen to have many wives, and Sylvia would be the newest and youngest of them. The other wives would order her about, and give her the hardest work to do, and they would despise her because she had never learnt their courtly skills of needlework and embroidery and playing upon the spinet. She was a farmer's daughter, not bred to court life. Poor Sylvia pleaded and pleaded with her father.

'Please don't make me go to marry the King. I want to stay here with you. I am happy here. Please ask the King to let me stay.'

'My beloved daughter,' said her father, weeping with her, 'I dare not oppose the King. He would have me thrown into a dungeon for insolence. He is known for his temper, if anyone goes against him. You wouldn't have your father pass the rest of his days in a black dungeon, would you? No, there is no other way. You must go with him. You will become a fine lady, with your own carriage. You may grow to enjoy the life. You will have prettier clothes than I will ever be able to buy for you and we will all come and visit you in the great castle.'

'I want none of that,' wailed Sylvia. 'I only want to stay here and be as I have always been. I will not go! I will not go!'

That night, the King and his men camped in the fields about the farm. When they rode away in the cold light of dawn, Sylvia rode with them, huddled in a huntsman's cloak, and followed closely by the King's bodyguard. The farm was full of shadows and the sound of weeping.

King Solander arranged a magnificent wedding, with a whole week of feasting and dancing, and Sylvia became his fourteenth wife. Poor girl, she felt lost amid all the glitter of lights and the chatter of courtly voices, and she longed for the quietness of her own home. The other wives soon began to bully her, and the King seemed to lose all interest in her after a few weeks. She was little better than a prisoner in the castle, for all her fine clothes and titles. Even the kitchen maids were better off than Sylvia; they had times off-duty when they could go about the town, or visit their families, but Sylvia was never free to do as she pleased. Almost every night, she cried herself to sleep, she was so unhappy. She would dream that she was at home with her beloved family, and then wakening was all the more bitter. When she thought of the years of sadness stretching out ahead of her, she was overwhelmed with grief. What could she do? Run away? No, there were soldiers all over the castle and the King's wives were closely guarded at all times. There seemed to be no hope for her until one day, when help came from a most unexpected place.

There was a wife called Marlanda. She had been the youngest wife until Sylvia had come. Now she could give Sylvia all the nasty jobs she'd had to do herself in the past. One day, Marlanda said to Sylvia, with a sneer, 'It's time you visited the dungeons, my dear. You haven't been yet, have you? No, well the King's forgotten you now, so it is no matter if you dirty your fine clothes. Here, take this to the deepest and smelliest dungeon you can find, and thrust it through the hatch in the door. Ask a guard to show you the way.'

She thrust a bundle of hay at Sylvia. A guard led her down and down, through cold stone passageways, down steep flights of steps, deep down into the cavernous roots of the castle. The deeper they went, the more filthy and smelly it became. Rats scuttled away ahead of them. The walls crawled with beetles and flies. Bats hung in dark corners. They reached the lowest depths at last. Sylvia was trying hard not to be sick. The guard said, 'I'll come no further, my lady. It's at the far end of the passage. A big oak door. Look out for poisonous snakes!' Roaring at his own joke, he clattered off back towards the fresh air, as quickly as he could go.

Sylvia now held her breath, and stepped in great fear towards the blackness at the end of the passage. Reaching the great door, she found a small hatch in it, opened it, and thrust the hay in as quickly as she could. She was just going to slam the hatch when a thought came to her. 'Who can it be, locked away in this dreadful place? Poor fellow, he must spend all his days here, and never see the sun.'

For the first time since she had entered the castle, Sylvia had forgotten her own troubles.

'Hallo, in there,' she called. 'Who are you?'

There was a rustling in the darkness, then a musty voice, sounding as though it had not spoken for years, said, 'Oh! Hello. Are you new, then? You're not allowed to talk to me, you know. No one is. They'll punish you. You'd better go away. Thanks for the hay.'

'It's all right,' said Sylvia. 'The guard's gone away. No one will hear me. Who are you?'

'Promise not to be afraid, if I tell you?'

'Promise.'

'I'm quite harmless. Nearly too weak to move, anyway. Cannot get strong on hay and rain water.'

'Well, who are you, then?' said Sylvia.

'I'm just a small one,' said the voice. 'Quite young, by our standards. Just a nipper, really.'

'But who are *you*?' said Sylvia.

'Well, as a matter of truth, I'm. . . well, my name's Wimble.'

'Are you a boy ?'

'No. I'm not human at all. I'm. . . well, I'm a very small dragon.'

'A dragon? Oh!' Sylvia *was* afraid and wondered if she should run for it.

'There, I knew you'd be afraid,' said Wimble. 'But I'm a good dragon. Strictly vegetarian.'

'What's that ?'

'It means I never eat meat. No, my family never could abide meat. We're not the sort of dragons to go eating maidens. We eat lettuces and cabbages; we munch up trees – fir-trees when we can get them, I love fir-trees.'

'Why are you in here, then?' asked Sylvia.

'That's an old story,' said Wimble. 'It was the

King's old dad that put me in here: Solander the First. He was just as bad as his son for wickedness. Well, I found some lovely fir-trees one day, on a hill not far from this castle, and I was munching away at them, and the King was out hunting and saw me. Well, I didn't know it was the King's forest. There was a notice, saying: ROYAL FOREST. KEEP OUT. TRESPASSERS WILL BE THROWN INTO THE ROYAL DUNGEONS FOREVER. But I cannot read, so I didn't know what it said. And when the King saw me, he called out his army, and caught me, and put me in here.'

'Forever?' said Sylvia, in horror.

'Yes. That's what he said. He read the notice out to me, and sentenced me on the spot. No good me saying I couldn't read. Same law for dragons as for men, he said. So there it is, and here I am.' Wimble began to cry in the darkness.

'Please don't cry, dear Wimble,' said Sylvia. 'I'll think of a way to get you out. We'll escape together. I'm nearly as much a prisoner as you are.' She went on to tell him her own sad tale, and all the time she was trying to think of a way they could escape. She thought of the pictures she had seen in books, and this gave her an idea.

'Wimble, can you fly?' she said.

'Yes, I have a lovely pair of wings. A bit stiff now, after all these years, though.'

'And can you breathe fire?'

'Yes, of course I can,' said Wimble proudly. 'Have to have a good drink of firewater first, of course.'

'Do you mean oil?' said Sylvia.

'Stuff you put in lamps.'

'Yes, I know.' Sylvia clapped her hands for glee. 'I fill the lamps in the King's apartments. I have a key to the oilstore.'

'What's the use?' said Wimble.

'You could burn this door down,' said Sylvia. 'It's made of wood. Then we could get away together. I can show you the quickest way out. You could blow fire at the guards and frighten them away. We could climb to the top of the castle. I'd climb on your back, and we'd fly far away together.'

'To my cave in the mountains.'

'Yes! Yes!'

'Oh, my mum and dad would be pleased to see me,' said Wimble. 'There's only one thing.'

'What's that?'

'I'm too weak to fly. I need feeding up. This hay's not enough to fly on. We'd just drop into the moat, and they'd pick us off with arrows.'

'I'll steal food for you,' said Sylvia. 'I can never eat my greens. I'll save them for you in a bag, and I'll steal more from the stores. Now that I know the way down here, I can come at night without being seen.'

'They'll put you in a dungeon, if they catch you,' said Wimble.

'I can't be much worse off than I am now,' said Sylvia. 'Anyway, they'll not catch me. I'll be specially careful. Are you willing to try my plan if I can get the oil and food for you?'

'Go on, then. Yes, I'll try it. Getting an arrow through my gizzard would be better than being stuck in here another fifty years. Dragons live a long time, you know, and they like to be free.'

'I'd better go back, now,' said Sylvia. 'They'll get suspicious if I'm too long. Goodbye.'

'Goodbye!'

Luckily for Sylvia, the guard who had brought her down had gone off duty, and a new one had taken his place, so he didn't know how long she'd been. Marlanda had also gone – to sing to the King as he ate his dinner – so all was well.

In the weeks that followed, Sylvia stole great quantities of oil and food for Wimble. She came to know the way to his dungeon so well that she could go in black darkness and never stumble. Wimble grew stronger and stronger. He became restless. One night he said to Sylvia, 'Let's go tonight. I'm sure I can fly now. Let's not wait any longer.'

'No, not yet,' said Sylvia. 'We must wait for a night with no moon. All good escapes are on moonless nights. We must plan this carefully. We only have one chance to do it, dear Wimble, and we *must* get away from this place.'

'I'm so tired of waiting,' grumbled Wimble.

'Patience, my friend. It will not be long. Can you make fire, yet?'

'I don't know.'

'Try just the tiniest puff. You mustn't start a blaze, or they'll soon smell us out. Can you? Just the least little bit?'

There was a sound of deep breathing, and a grunting. Then, a little blue flame appeared in the darkness. The flame grew until it was as long as Sylvia's arm.

'Quick, put it out!' she said.

Wimble sucked the flame in and put it out with a pop.

'That's lovely,' said Sylvia. 'And, Wimble – do you know, it's the first time I've seen you. I could see quite clearly by the light of your flame. You never told me how beautiful you are. Your scales shine like a sunset.'

'Oh, well. . .' said Wimble. 'Anyway, I could say the same about you, but I always knew you were beautiful, I could tell by your voice, and your kindness in helping a poor dragon.'

'We know you can burn the door down, now. What about your wings ?'

'There isn't enough room in here to stretch

them properly. We'll just have to see when we get out.'

'Oh. . . yes. . .I do hope you can fly. Now we only have a week to wait for a moonless night. I asked the astrologer. So be patient a little longer.' With this, Sylvia crept back to bed.

Something happened next day that changed all their careful plans. The King's Treasurer sent for Sylvia.

'I've been going over the accounts,' he said, 'and we've used twenty-three barrels of lamp-oil during the month of April. Never before have we used more than five! What has happened to the missing eighteen barrels?'

'I . . . I don't know, sir,' said Sylvia, blushing.

'You do fill the lamps, don't you?'

'Yes, it's been my job ever since I came.'

'So you must know how we can have used so much oil. Come now, there's been no banquet, or all night feast, has there?'

'No,' said Sylvia, in a small voice, trying to hide her thoughts from this sharp-eyed man.

'Have you sold it to some fool, to fill your pockets with gold?'

'No, I have not,' said Sylvia loudly. 'I would never do such a dishonest thing.'

'Then what *have* you done with it, child? I don't suppose you've been drinking it! Well, if you'll not tell me, the King will make you tell.

He has ways that never fail. This matter must be cleared up and I'll not be blamed for it. I'll go to the King now. Now – will you tell me, or not?'

'I cannot tell you,' said Sylvia, quite truthfully.

'Then I'll go to the King. You'll be sorry for this, young lady.' With this, the angry Treasurer swept off to the King's audience chamber, leaving Sylvia trembling with fear of what might happen. But luck was on her side again. The King was away at a tournament and the matter would have to wait until the next day.

That night, as soon as she was sure everyone was asleep, Sylvia crept down to the dungeons. This time she took a whole barrel of oil.

'Wimble,' she called, 'are you awake?'

'Hello! Yes, here I am, but you're early. The tower clock's only struck one o'clock.'

'Yes, I know. Listen, something's happened. We must flee at once.' She told him all about her meeting with the Treasurer. 'If I'm still here tomorrow, the King will have me tortured, and then I'll have to tell him everything, and all will be over.'

'At once?' said Wimble. 'You mean this very night?'

'Yes. Yes.'

'Oh dear, I'm not sure I can. I don't feel very fiery.'

'You must,' said Sylvia. 'Look, I've brought you a whole barrel of oil.'

Wimble drank the oil greedily. Then he licked his lips.

'That was good,' he said. 'I feel a real dragon, now. Stand well clear of the door. It's now or never, I see. Stand back! I'm going to burn it down!'

Sylvia retreated up the passage. There was a sound of blowing, rather like the sighing of a big pair of bellows. A blue light shone out, then bright yellow flame suddenly blossomed within Wimble's dungeon. Vicious tongues of it spurted all round the door, and the wood began to crackle and burn. The iron hinges twisted in the heat. More and more flame gushed out. Then, there was a shuddering crash, and Wimble came crashing through the door, scattering sparks and smoke like some amazing firework.

'Quick,' cried Sylvia. 'Follow me!'

Shouts of 'Fire! Fire!' were heard in the upper parts of the castle and people began tumbling sleepily out of their beds. Sylvia and Wimble fled along the stone passages and up flight after flight of stairs. Wimble had drawn his fire in, but his nostrils still showed sparks. At the first door leading to the open air they met four soldiers with spears.

'Stop, or we'll kill you,' the soldiers shouted. Wimble shot a long tongue of flame at them. They dropped their spears, and ran for it, with the seats of their trousers badly scorched. Out on to the open battlements went Sylvia and Wimble, climbing higher and higher. All the castle was in turmoil now. The women ran screaming, 'Fire! Fire! We'll be roasted in our beds!' The men searched for swords and bows, and some in their hurry put their armour on back-to-front so that they couldn't even walk. Ten more soldiers tried to stop Sylvia and Wimble but another puff of fire sent them running.

Then Sylvia saw the firemen with their buckets of water and their big water-squirts.

'Quickly, Wimble. They'll put your fire out!' she screamed. 'Spread your wings!'

They were perched on the highest battlement. Sylvia climbed on to Wimble's back and clung on grimly. Wimble opened his wings. Oh, how they creaked!

'Ouch!' groaned Wimble. 'My wing-muscles are so stiff. I don't think I can fly at all.'

'Oh Wimble, you must. Look, the bowmen are coming – hundreds of them, with arrows ready for us. And the firemen will put out your flames.

Jump, Wimble, jump!'

Making a desperate effort, Wimble forced his wings to open. Then, he jumped from the battlements. Still his wings would not flap. They plunged down, down, falling towards the deep moat. As they passed the lower parts of the castle, the bowmen loosed their arrows, and the wicked shafts reached out for them. Sylvia felt the breath of them, flying past. She held on, and closed her eyes tightly, and spoke to Wimble.

'Try, Wimble, try. All the arrows missed, but we'll drown if we fall in the moat. Wimble, you *must* fly!'

At the last moment, Wimble's wings began to beat. Sylvia felt their fall slow down. Then they were hovering just above the dark water. Then they began to lift up, up into the free air. The ground swayed, and began to drop away. A shouting squad of bowmen ran out of the castle and began to shoot at them, but the arrows fell harmlessly back to earth.

'Wimble, we're out of bowshot,' Sylvia called out. 'We're winning. The arrows cannot reach us. We've done it!'

The dragon was too busy to answer, but his wings beat more and more strongly now, and the castle and town began to slip away below them, becoming smaller and smaller. Wimble circled higher and higher, and at last the light of sunrise could be seen on the far horizon. He rested, gliding gently on his widely spread wings.

'Look,' he said to Sylvia. 'The mountains of home that I never dared hope to see again. Oh, how can I ever thank you....' Wimble was so overcome that big dragon tears welled from his eyes, and people on the earth below were amazed to feel large drops of hot, salty rain falling.

'How can I thank *you* ?' said Sylvia. 'We could not have done it without each other. See, there's my father's farm, away below your right wing. What a dear sight it is.'

'I will fly you there soon,' said Wimble. 'But first we must deal with King Solander, so that he will never trouble either of us again.'

When Wimble reached his home cave in the wild mountains, there was great joy. His mother and father, his grandfather and grandmother, his great-grandfather and great-grandmother, and his six brothers and six sisters, all rushed out to greet Wimble with tears and laughter and little spurts of coloured flame. They didn't know that Wimble had been in King Solander's dungeon for fifty years past, and they had long ago given him up for dead, thinking some giant must have killed and eaten him. Yet here he was, alive and well! Wimble introduced Sylvia to them all, and told them the full story of the wonderful escape he and Sylvia had planned. The whole dragon family sat round and listened in an admiring silence. Then, old Zachary, Wimble's great-grandfather, and a magnificent dragon of fearsome size, rose in agitation to his feet.

'My dear little Wimble,' he said. 'There is no time to lose. This is a good tale you tell, but we must stop Solander before his soldiers can reach the farm of Sylvia's father. I know that wicked King of old; he will certainly burn the farm and throw the whole family into the dungeons, in revenge for your escape, if he doesn't kill them at once.'

'Oh!' cried Sylvia, going pale.

'Never fear, my child,' said Zachary, 'we dragons will not allow that to happen. You have brought our beloved Wimble back to us and we will be your friends forever. We are a peaceful family, and have lived quietly here for many thousands of years. We never want to fight the tribes of men; we go our ways and they go theirs. But if they attack us with armies, then we will fight to defend ourselves and the world will see us again in all our ferocity. We will smash their castles and spew fire upon their armies.' As he said this, black smoke began to pour from his nostrils, and he was a terrible sight. 'Even now, King Solander will be mustering his armies to march against us, and he will never rest until he has Wimble's head upon the point of his sword.

No, Wimble, do not be afraid. We will go out to battle, and settle King Solander and his army forever. Have no fear, we will all live in peace after this battle. Enough of words! Dragons arise! It is war! War upon King Solander and all his works!'

As Zachary's call to battle thundered about the mountains, all nineteen dragons spread their wings, and rose into the air. Sylvia rode on Wimble's back. On the way, the dragons swooped down to drink from a lake of oil, and each one picked up an enormous rock in his talons. Then they flew on, towards Solander's castle.

It was a short battle. The dragons flew high over the castle. Zachary was the first to drop his rock. It was the biggest by far – the size of a cottage – and it smashed into the castle with a fearful grinding and tearing of wood and stone. Down it smashed, down through the attics, down through the bedrooms and boudoirs and bathrooms; nothing could stop it. It was a lucky aim indeed. As the great rock smashed its way into the heart of the castle, King Solander was sitting on his throne, conducting a Council of War with his generals. The rock fell exactly on the throne. One moment, the King was sitting there in all his battle array; the next moment, he was gone, throne and all! There was a gaping hole in the floor. The generals ran away in terror, thinking some magical spell had been laid upon Solander. Down and down the rock went, taking the King with it; down through storerooms and dungeons, until it reached the bed-rock of the castle's foundations, where it finally stopped for ever. King Solander was never seen again and no trace of him was ever found. In later years, an inscription was carved on the rock, telling of the downfall of the wicked King Solander, and parties came from all over the land to see it and wonder at it.

The other dragons dropped their smaller rocks, smashing down the towers and turrets of the castle. They swooped low over the castle, breathing fire, and all that would burn was reduced to ash. There was no need for fighting after this. With King Solander dead, and all his power in ruins, his soldiers and servants threw their arrows and spears and armour into the flames, and went back to their farms and their families. King Solander was the only one who died in the battle, and the people were full of joy when they heard of this, for now they were free from the harsh poverty that his rule had brought them. There was an end to the fighting that Solander had loved so much; the people were free to grow good food, and live peacefully on their land.

The dragon family flew away to their home in the mountains, and the people never saw them again. On the way, Wimble took Sylvia back to her father's farm. Her mother and father, and brothers and sisters, were overjoyed to see her, though they were terrified to see her arriving on the back of a real dragon. Such a tale she had to tell them, of all her adventures; but she soon forgot the sadness of her days as a queen and lived as happily as before. When the sun rose over the wild mountains, she often thought of Wimble, and wondered if he was as happy with his family as she was with hers.

Eight

King Calamy and the dragon's egg

It was in the time of King Calamy the First that the Royal Dragon grew too old to fight.

'The poor old thing's so old that he cannot even run, never mind fly or spurt fire,' said King Calamy to his Queen. 'His days of glory are over. If we had to do battle with anyone, he'd surely be killed, and what a disgrace that would be. Whatever shall we do?'

'Quite simple, my love,' said the Queen. 'Get a new dragon and put the old one out to grass.'

'Get a new dragon? A *new* one? And where in the kingdom do you suggest I should find a new dragon, my sweet?' demanded the King. 'You seem to forget that we have had old Krog for nine hundred and ninety-nine years! Things were very different in the old days, when King Rongob caught Krog as a baby dragon, and brought him here to be tamed and taught to fight our enemies. There were more dragons about then - the history books are full of them.

They're a dying race, my dear; a thing of the past!'

'Nonsense,' said the Queen. 'Only last week, young Lord Pango came back from a hunting trip saying he'd heard stories about dragon's eggs being seen somewhere.'

'Eggs!' said the King, a light coming into his eyes. 'Eggs. The very thing. Why didn't I think of it? Eggs. Eggs.'

'What are you rambling on about now?' asked the Queen. 'You've surely heard of eggs before?'

'Yes, of course I have, but I didn't think of them as an answer to the dragon problem. I forgot that they take so long to hatch. Don't you see? If we can find a dragon's egg, we can bring it back here and hatch it out! So much easier than catching a young dragon in some wild spot and bringing it home. An egg cannot run away or escape; it cannot bite or burn. A dragon's egg! We must find a dragon's egg. Quick, now, where did you say Pango heard of these eggs?'

'Oh. . . somewhere.'

'I know it was *somewhere*, woman, can't you be more exact than that? I can't tell my knights to go and search "somewhere" for a dragon's egg, now can I?'

'Oh, I don't know,' said the Queen vaguely; 'it was in some wild place. Why don't you ask Pango himself? I wasn't listening properly when he talked of it. I was wondering if you could make an omelette with such an egg.'

'Omelettes indeed!' shouted the King. 'Just like a woman. Send for Lord Pango! Send him to me at once! I must have words with him.'

Lord Pango was summoned. He had a long talk with the King, and there was much unrolling of maps, and deep considering over cup after cup of coffee, and the end of it was that Lord Pango set out a week later at the head of an expedition.

There was great excitement in the city when Lord Pango set out. Cheering crowds lined the

streets all the way to the North Gate. There were twenty knights in armour, with their squires, and a long baggage-train of mules, carrying all the tents and food and weapons needed for a long and dangerous journey into the wild mountainous country to the north, far from the safety of the city walls. There were fierce enemy tribes roaming the countryside and Lord Pango and his men might have to stand and fight. Most important of all, they carried a magnificent casket, in which to carry the precious egg home. It rode in a beautiful palanquin, covered in cloth-of-gold, and carried by four white horses, amid the glittering spears of the knights.

The last person to wave Lord Pango on his way was David, a boy who lived on a farm half a day's ride from the city. David's father kept hens and ducks and geese and David helped with all the work of the farm. Once a week, he rode to market in the city, with two great baskets slung on his horse, full of eggs; small hens' eggs; larger duck eggs; still larger goose eggs. These he sold in the market. So he heard all the gossip of the people of the city, and knew all about Lord Pango's expedition, for the city was all a'chatter about it.

'God speed! And a safe return!' he called after the knights. He gazed in wonder at the golden palanquin, and marvelled that such a costly thing should be made to carry a single egg.

Lord Pango and his knights travelled far. After many weary weeks, they found what they sought. On a wild peak of the Shivering Mountains, lodged behind a boulder, almost out of sight, was a real dragon's egg, creamy white and crimson veined. With trembling hands, they lifted it into the casket, wrapped it in soft silken cloths, and placed it gently in the golden palanquin. Then they made for home, with all speed. They were about half way home, when a roving band of Malandrian knights spotted the glinting of the sun upon their golden palanquin. The

Malandrian knights hid by the track in a narrow mountain pass and laid an ambush. When Lord Pango and his men came past, the Malandrians fell upon them with fierce battle cries, and took Lord Pango and all his proud knights prisoner without a fight, so great and sudden was their surprise. The dragon's egg was broken in the turmoil of the battle, and the Malandrians were greatly surprised when they looked inside the casket in the golden palanquin; expecting to find gold and jewels, they found only the mess of the broken egg. Malagorn, their leader, was very angry.

'What is this?' he shouted. 'What is this mess? Where are your amethysts and sapphires? Where is your gold and silver ? Come now, we know you come to the mountains to seek treasure. Tell me where it is, or you die, every man of you.'

Lord Pango fell on his knees before Malagorn.

'I beg you, my lord,' he said, 'not to kill us, for it is against the laws of knighthood. Upon my honour as a knight, I swear to you that that *is* our treasure you see there. It is, or was, an egg.'

'An egg? What madness is this? A band of knights out to seek an egg?'

'Yes, my lord. Our King, Calamy the First, has taken a sudden desire to have a certain very rare egg for his collection.'

'What is its use?'

'It's use, sir? Why, sir, none that I know of. It is only that his collection is not complete without it.'

'Your King sounds a fool to me, but I almost believe your silly story. However – no harm in searching you. Men! Search them! And if a single jewel is found, I will blunt my sword on your bones.'

Every man was searched. Nothing was found. The Malandrians scowled in disappointment and climbed on their horses.

'To tell the truth,' said Malagorn, 'we need horses more than we need jewels. So we're taking yours. You'll have a long walk home. Farewell!'

Grinning now, they rode off, leaving Lord Pango and his men without a single horse between them.

For many days, Lord Pango's expedition trudged wearily across the wild countryside, each man laden with heavy armour, and tents, and the great sacks of food that the horses had carried. They were lucky enough not to be attacked again but they were a sorry sight when they reached the North Gate of the city, five weeks later. Their clothes were in tatters and the golden palanquin was spattered all over with mud.

King Calamy was told of their arrival. When he saw them, he said, 'What in the world have you been doing all this time? Just look at you! What have you done with your horses? Where's the dragon's egg? Quick, show it to me.'

Silently, Lord Pango lifted the lid of the casket. The King saw a mass of broken shell and a dreadful smell made him bang the lid down again.

'Is – was – that it ?' he said.

'Yes,' said Lord Pango sadly, and told the King the whole story.

'Well, what are we going to do now?' said King Calamy.

'Send another expedition,' said the Queen.

So he did. The same thing happened again, but this time they were attacked by another war-band, who smashed their palanquin to pieces, and stole the casket.

'It's the palanquin and casket that attracts the brigands,' said the Queen. 'Send an expedition without these things.'

So King Calamy sent an expedition with a plain wooden box to collect the egg in, but they were attacked and put to flight before they even reached the mountains. By now, all the wandering bands of knights knew that King Calamy was trying to get a dragon's egg for hatching, for rumour and gossip had carried the news all over the land. They were determined to stop him, because they knew that a new dragon would be a great danger to them. King Calamy sent out more expeditions, but every one of them was attacked as soon as it was well clear of the safety of the city walls. Soon, it became dangerous for any soldier or knight to leave the city at all and King Calamy despaired of ever getting a dragon's egg.

Then, the Queen had another idea.

'Why not offer a prize to anyone who can bring a dragon's egg safely to the city ?'

'Why not?' said the King. 'It's our last chance. Our enemies will attack the city soon if we don't get a new dragon. Yes, we'll do it.'

So the heralds proclaimed a prize of one thousand gold pieces for anyone who brought a good dragon's egg safely to the King. This gave David an idea in his turn – David, the boy who brought his father's eggs to market: brown hens' eggs; big duck eggs; still bigger goose eggs.

One day, instead of riding to town with his big baskets of eggs, he turned his horse towards the mountains. He carried simple provisions; bread and cheese, and a gourd of wine; and a small pan to cook eggs in. He soon met a roving band of knights, who were on the lookout for the King's expeditions.

'Who are you, and what is your business? What have you got in those baskets?' demanded their leader.

'I am David. My father has a small farm, with hens, ducks and geese. My baskets are full of eggs. I am on my way to the city beyond the mountains to sell my eggs for I can get a better price there than in King Calamy's city. The people are poor there. All their money is spent in taxes, to pay for fruitless expeditions.'

The knight grinned at this and said, 'Go on your way boy. We have no quarrel with honest traders, or with duck eggs.'

And they let David go, unharmed. As he went on his way, he met many more bands of knights, and the same thing happened each time. When he reached the mountains, it was quieter, and he camped out many a night without seeing anyone. Then, he began to hunt for dragons' eggs. If he met anyone, he pretended simply to be travelling on towards the distant city, so that no one knew of his real quest. After many days of seeking, David was rewarded. He found a beautiful dragon egg, nestling under some broad ferns. It was marked all over with fine crimson lines – the one sure sign of a dragon egg, as he knew. He took some chalk-dust from a pouch on his belt, and rubbed it all over the egg, making it white. Now it looked just like a goose egg, even if it was a little bit larger. He lifted a number of goose eggs out of one of his baskets, made a space, and gently placed the dragon egg in it. Then he covered it over with a good deep layer of goose eggs. He turned his horse round and headed back for home.

On the way back, David met many more bands of knights. Some looked suspiciously into his basket but they all let him go on. It was quite obvious that he really was a seller of eggs, an innocent trader with no notions about dragons. David's worst moment was when he met a band of hungry knights, who were luckily honest, and bought what they could easily have taken from him. They bought all his hen eggs, and all his duck eggs, and would have bought his goose eggs too, but he said, 'These eggs are for hatching, not eating, and so more costly. My father will beat me if I don't take them safely home; he hopes to hatch a great many geese for the Christmas fairs. Good, sir knights, please let me keep my goose eggs.'

The knights laughed and their leader said, 'He shall keep his geese. Go on your way, boy, we'll not earn you a beating.'

And so David came to the city gates at last, and went to the palace to tell King Calamy of his quest, and claim his reward.

'Is it possible?' said King Calamy, looking in amazement at the basket of goose eggs. 'Is it possible that a boy has succeeded where all my soldiers and brave knights have failed? Are you pulling my leg boy? Come now, are you? It doesn't do to tease a king. I could have your head chopped off, just like that! You have dozens of eggs there.'

'No, sire, it is true; I have brought you a dragon egg. If you will send for a bowl of water, I will show you.'

'Water? A bowl of water? The boy's crazy.'

'Humour him,' said the Queen. 'Let's see what his game is.'

Turning to a footman, she said, 'Water. A bowl of water, at once.'

The water was brought. David knelt before the King. He took his eggs from the basket, one by one. He washed each one carefully in the water, and laid it on the grass. He could not guess himself, so good was the disguise which was the dragon egg; but he came at last to an egg that revealed a pattern of fine crimson lines when it was washed. He held it out to the King, in triumph.

'For you, your majesty. One dragon's egg. May I have my reward?'

'Indeed it is,' whispered the King. 'I have seen it just so, in my book of eggs. My boy, how did you do it, with the fields full of armed knights and brigands?'

'It was simple,' said David. 'I carry eggs to

market every week. People are used to seeing me with baskets of eggs, so no one takes any notice when I pass by. When your knights march past with their glittering armour and bright flags, everyone notices, the word runs before them, and the enemy are on the lookout. No matter how your knights carried a dragon's egg, it would be found and destroyed. What better place to hide an egg than amongst a lot of other eggs?'

'No better place in all the world,' laughed the King. 'The boy has more brains than the rest of us put together. Give him the thousand gold pieces – he's earned them.'

David returned home rich and famous. The egg was hatched, and a fine new dragon came out of it, and King Calamy's city was safe for another nine-hundred years.

Nine

Inside outside

There was once a man called Robert Cropper, and he was walking along the side of Pendle Hill one very dark night, when he found what he thought was a very big cave.

'That's funny,' he said to himself, 'I never knew there was a cave on Pendle Hill.'

Now he was out, with his gun on his arm, hunting a fox that had stolen three of his ducks. Thinking the fox could be hiding in there, he stepped softly and silently into the cave. There were some sharp rocks sticking up in a row all across the floor, and more sticking down from the roof, so he stepped carefully over and between them, and got inside with no trouble. Now it was very dark in there; so dark that he couldn't see out of his eyeballs at all. So he felt his way along, deeper into the cave. It was a queer cave. The floor was soft and squashy and slithery and Robert could not tell why it should be so. The walls, too, were the same way. There was a wind in there, too. But such a queer wind!

First it blew out of the cave, then it blew in. Out and in, out and in, the wind came to and fro. Outside it was a freezing cold night, but in the cave it was warm, so Robert loosened his coat and scarf. He went on into the cave, and he could feel the floor beginning to slope downwards, more and more steeply. He was just thinking he'd better turn back, when his feet flew up into the black air and he sat down hard. Then he was sliding! He was slipping and sliding down and down, faster and faster! The slope became steep and he whizzed along in the dark! Desperately he snatched and grabbed with his hands, trying to catch hold of something that would stop him, but there was nothing to hold, nothing but slippery surfaces that skimmed by under his fingers.

'Help!' he shouted. 'He. . .lp!'

But there was no one to hear him. Now he shook with fear, and as he skated along, he began to cry and blubber like a child. Where was he going? How would he ever get out of this alive? If this went on, he would surely fall right down into the fires in the middle of the earth.

Then the slope began to flatten out, and Robert slowed down. There was a glow of light ahead, far down a dimly seen tunnel.

'Thank Heaven! I can see again,' said Robert.

'But where in the world, or out of it, am I?'

As he slid on, the light became brighter, and he could see the tunnel more clearly. It was round, and red, and smooth. It curved gently to the right, and the light was out of sight round the corner, but grew quickly brighter. Then Robert rounded the corner, and came out into.an enormous cavern, lit by a great many little lights. Suddenly, he bumped against something hard, and stopped.

Robert sat where he was for a while taking in what he saw before him. The cavern was full of large shadowy shapes; big square things, with fuzzy tops, that sloped up to a ridge. At first they seemed like strange monsters standing about. Then they seemed stranger still, when Robert saw what ordinary things they were to find in such a weird place. They were cottages, just like the ones in his own village, with thatched roofs. They were scattered about the floor of the cave, just as if they had been thrown there, instead of being in the straight lines of proper streets. The lights were candles, shining in their windows.

'A town under the earth!' said Robert, in a whisper. 'It must be the home of the little-folks, or the pixies, or some such, that my granny used to tell me about. I hope they're good fairies, and

125

that they'll help me to get back to my dear home again.'

He got carefully to his feet, went up to the nearest door, and knocked on it. The door opened, and there was an old fairy with a grizzled beard, saying, 'Well, well, here's a visitor at last from the outside world. Well, now, you're a right welcome sight. Come in, and tell us what's going on, and how you got here, and how they're going to rescue us.'

Robert hesitated on the doorstep.

'What kind of fairy are you?' he said.

'Fairy?' said the bearded one. 'Fairy? I'm no more a fairy than your grandmother, you foolish fellow. I'm a man like yourself, can't you see?'

'Oh,' said Robert. 'Yes, I thought. . . But. . . oh, dear, I'm all in a muddle. I thought this was the magical kingdom under the earth, and you must be the little people.'

'Nonsense,' said the man. 'Are you drunk or something ? Don't you know where you are?'

'No.'

'You're inside the dragon.'

'Inside the *what*?'

'Inside the dragon.'

'Which dragon?'

'The dragon that swallowed us, and our whole village; cottages, church, pub, school and all.'

'I never saw any dragon,' said Robert.

'Is it dark outside?' said the man.

'Yes.'

'Where were you, before you came here?'

'I was walking on Pendle Hill, looking for foxes.'

'Did you walk into anything? I mean, did you go inside anything?'

'Yes. I stepped into a big cave.'

'Did you slide down a slippery place?'

'Yes.'

'That was no cave you stepped into.'

'What was it?' asked Robert, his heart suddenly cold within him.

'It was the dragon's mouth. He sleeps with his mouth open, because he has a cold, and his nose is stuffed up. He must have fallen asleep on that hill of yours, and you just walked into him, in the dark. Couldn't you feel a wind blowing in and out?'

'Yes.'

'There you are, then. That was his breathing.'

'So I really am inside a dragon?' said Robert, trembling. 'You really are,' said the bearded man. 'But don't be afraid. He can't crunch you up, now you're inside and past his teeth.'

'But how can I get out?' wailed Robert.

'That's just it,' said the man, 'you can't. At least we haven't found a way out yet, and we've been two weeks in here. We're getting short of food and drink and I don't know what we're going to do. But come on in; we cannot talk on the doorstep all night. My name's Tom Cocker, and this is my dear wife, Mary.'

Robert stepped into the cottage, and shook hands with a grey-haired old lady, who asked them to sit down and have a sup of cider. Then Tom Cocker told the whole story, as they drank.

'Something had upset this dragon, you see, and he came rampaging out of Scotland one morning, in a dreadful temper, and the first place he comes to, as he gallops over the Cheviot Hills, is Humbleton, our own village itself, close by Humbleton Hill. Well, he begins to eat the sheep on the hill, and young Aidan Thompson goes running out to shout at him, because they're Aidan's sheep, you see. His wife Dorothy tells him it's no good, shouting at a dragon, but there's no stopping him, and he shouts every insult he can think of at the dragon. So the dragon gets angrier than ever. So what does it do? It opens its great jaws, and swallows the whole village, with all the people in it! So here we are, all alive and well, because in his hurry the dragon swallowed us whole, without chewing, and I should think we're giving him a dreadful stomach ache.'

'And serve him right, too,' said Mary.

'Couldn't we climb out again, whilst he's asleep?' said Robert.

'It's too slippery up his throat,' said Tom.

'We've tried many times, but we just slip back again.'

'But we'll starve to death, if we stay here,' said Robert. 'We must get out. There must be a way.'

'You're a clever man if you can find it,' said Tom. 'We've all despaired.'

'So this is not a cave at all, but the inside of a dragon's stomach?' said Robert.

'Yes,' said Tom.

'A big dragon. Perhaps the biggest in the world,' said Robert, thinking hard. 'Will you show me all round it, as far as we can go, safely?'

'Surely,' said Tom. 'I'll light my lantern and we'll go for a walk.'

So Tom and Robert set out together, with the lantern throwing its light upon the red walls of the dragon's stomach. They went first to the dragon's gullet where Robert had come sliding down. Tom held his lantern up to see it, and it was like looking up the inside of some gigantic chimney. Robert tried to climb up, but he soon slithered back, for there was nothing at all to hold on to.

'You're right, it's no good that way,' he said. 'Let's have a look at the other end.'

So they walked the length of the dragon's

stomach, past the cottages, all jumbled about, just as they had been gulped down, with their winking candles. At the widest part, they couldn't see the roof of the stomach; the lantern's light just faded away into the gloom. Then, as they went on, the stomach grew narrower, and its roof and walls could be seen again. Still they went on. The stomach tapered away gradually; it was like walking into a funnel. They went on until there was just enough room to walk side by side. Tom stopped.

'This is the farthest I've been,' he said. 'It's no good going any farther. It just gets narrower and we might get stuck.'

'Wait a minute,' said Robert. 'We've come so far, we must surely be inside the dragon's tail by now?'

'Yes, I suppose so.'

'Well, I mean to go on. There isn't room for two, so I'll go alone. Will you lend me your lantern?'

'You'll only get stuck,' said Tom. 'Then Mary'll blame me, and if the dragon starts galloping it will thrash its tail about and knock you to pieces.'

'I've had an idea; I must go on,' said Robert stubbornly.

'There's no way out down its tail, you daft fellow,' said Tom, laughing; 'but I see there's no stopping you. You'll just have to see for yourself. Here you are. I'll go back by candle-light.'

So he gave Robert the lantern, and Robert went forward, holding it out in front of him. The dragon's tail soon closed in upon him, and it was not long before he was pushing himself along the narrowing tube, like a cork in a bottle. Tighter and tighter the inside of the tail squeezed him, but Robert squeezed his shoulders together, made his body as small as he could, and pressed farther and farther, tighter and tighter.

'What if I *should* get stuck? Will they be able to pull me out?' he thought.

But he pushed onward, because he wanted to find the end, the very end of the inside of this enormous dragon's long, long tail. Then, just when he thought he must go back or stick fast for ever, he saw what he had been praying for – a great bone, with a hole in it, that made it look like a ring, the size of a mill-stone! He had reached the end! Now he saw this odd bone, he remembered what he had once seen as a small child, over by Noyna Rocks. He had seen a bone just like this one, bleached white in the sun, and his grandfather had said, 'That bone comes from inside the end of a dragon's tail. They do say another dragon bit it off in a fight, and left it there.'

It must have been that dim memory that had

led him on, to push his way down that fearsome tunnel. But now he saw the bone, and the hole in it, his idea grew bigger. He must get back, quickly, to tell Tom and the other villagers. Oh, what a struggle Robert had! He tugged and pulled; he dug his elbows into the tail's sides, and wedged his way backwards, oh so slowly. But gradually the space became wider again and Robert speeded up. At last he could turn round, then he raced back to the stomach.

When Robert reached the stomach again, he came popping out of the tail at such a speed that he ran full into Tom Cocker, who was waiting anxiously for him, and knocked him over. What a gasping there was, and the two of them talking at once, and picking each other up, and falling over each other in their haste! When they had sorted themselves out, Robert told Tom all that he had seen. Then he told him his plan of escape. Tom looked full of astonishment and disbelief.

'You must be mad,' he said. 'It will never work.'

'It's our only chance,' said Robert, 'so it's worth trying. Come now, you said you knew no other way, so why not try mine? Come on, let's try it.'

'Oh, well. Very well, I'll help you.'

'There's a good fellow, I knew you would. Now

the first thing is ropes. We need a lot of strong rope.'

'We can use the bell-ropes from the church,' said Tom. 'And the blacksmith should have some good coils of rope, too.'

They set to work, and by the next day they had collected a large pile of ropes, and they knotted them all together with the best knots they knew. Then Robert tied the end of this long rope round his waist, took the lantern, and went off into the tail again. A crowd soon gathered, and they watched in amazement as the rope uncoiled and went snaking off into the inside of the tail.

'Whatever are you doing?' said Reg Post. 'Have you gone stark raving mad?'

'Just you wait and see, and be ready to help when the time comes, and you may yet see the sky again,' said Tom. The crowd gave a little cheer at that thought, and waited in quiet excitement to see what would happen.

When Robert reached the tail's end again, he untied the rope from his waist, pushed it through the hole in the bone, and tied it fast. Then he edged and elbowed his way back again. Back in the stomach, he shouted, 'I've done it! Now pull! Pull for your lives!'

Led by Tom and Robert, all the people, men, women and children, took a grip on the rope.

'We want a steady pull, not a jerk,' said

Robert. 'Now, when I count three, all heave together. One . . . Two. . . Three . . . Heave! And again! *heave*!'

The rope twanged and tightened and took the strain. As all two hundred of them pulled steadily, the rope slowly began to come out of the tail's tunnel! More and more came, and the people backed slowly across the stomach, pulling as they went.

'The rope's not broken, but it's coming out!' shouted Reg. 'What's happening?'

'Don't you know?' asked Robert, dancing with glee. 'Look!'

The end of the tail came into sight, with the rope tied round the dragon's bone.

'Impossible!' shouted Tom. 'We're doing it! We're doing it! *We're turning the dragon inside-out!*' And he danced for glee. 'Keep pulling! Don't stop!'

Now all the people began to grin for joy, and they pulled with renewed strength upon the rope. They pulled and pulled; more and more of the inside-out tail came out into the stomach, stretching across the swallowed village. When the end of the tail reached the dragon's gullet, Robert untied the rope, and tied it again near to the tail's root. Then they all began to pull again, but beginning now to turn the dragon's *body* inside-out!

If the scene inside the dragon was strange, it seemed stranger still to one who watched *outside!* A shepherd out on the mountain with his flock that morning, saw a longtailed dragon, quietly sleeping on the mountain, one moment; the next its tail began to disappear! Soon it was all gone, and the end of its body began to follow. Then the end of the inside-out tail was seen to poke out of the dragon's mouth! At this point the dragon woke up. Seeing its tail to be gone, it began to roar in anger. It tried to clash its jaws, but could not because its own tail was in the way. Then a man appeared in the dragon's mouth, climbing up the tail. When he reached the end, he jumped to the ground. A second man appeared on the tail and threw a rope's end down. The first man (it was Robert) ran with it to a tree, and tied it to the broad trunk. Then the other man, Tom, jumped down, and another man came up the tail, and another, and another, and another, until a crowd stood by the rope. Then women and children came climbing out, until the whole village stood on the grass. All this time the dragon was roaring and screaming most horribly, but it could not bite anyone. Then the people grasped the rope, and all pulled and pulled together. The dragon dug its claws into the grass, and pulled the other way, not knowing that this would only help the people. Suddenly there was a loud tearing sound, and a last scream from the dragon, and the rope came out so quickly that the people tumbled over in a heap; but when they picked themselves up, they saw that the dragon was dead, and completely inside-out! It was the queerest and most disgusting sight in all the world. But they were delighted to see that their cottages had all tumbled out of the dragon, too. So as soon as they had set them the right way up, they made a new village beside Pendle Hill, and never went home to Humbleton again. The rope was still tied to the dragon, so they dragged it round to the other side of the hill, where the wild creatures soon picked the bones clean.

This is the only inside-out dragon in all history. If you go to Humbleton, in Northumberland, today, you can still see the foundations where those dragon-swallowed cottages once stood.

Ten

The very greedy monster

Once there was a Monster. He lived far away on an island. He was very big, and very strong, and very greedy. He was so big, and so strong, that none of the other creatures could fight him. He was so greedy, that wanting something and getting it, were the same thing to him. So he grew bigger, and stronger, and greedier, with each day that passed. He had a wonderful life. He ate what he liked. He did what he liked. He played with whoever he liked; the other animals were so afraid of him, that if he shouted, 'Come and play with me!' they just had to. But to be friends with Monster, or to play with him, was just as dangerous as fighting him, as you will see.

One day, Monster was playing at racing along the beach with three antelopes. Now antelopes can run very fast, but they ran slowly, to let Monster win. They knew he would be angry if he didn't win. So the first race, the second race, and the third race, Monster won easily. This made him proud, and he strutted about, bellowing, 'See what a fine Monster I am! I can race you silly antelopes, easy as easy. Pooh, I could race you backwards!'

This was too much for Tappo, the youngest of the antelopes. 'That's not *fair!*' he shouted. 'Give us one more race and we'll show you.'

'Hush. Hush,' said the other antelopes, trembling with fear.

'I'll race you any day,' said Monster. 'Backwards, forwards, upside-down, legs tied together, any way you like!'

'We challenge you to an ordinary forwards race,' said Tappo, refusing to be hushed.

'Very well,' said Monster. 'One, two. . .' he began counting, then he was off before the antelopes, and shouting over his shoulder, 'three, GO!' Now the antelopes were so angry at this cheating, that this time they ran as fast as they could. Their legs moved at such speed that they were just a blur. They soon caught up with Monster, who was wallowing along in the sand. Then they passed him and reached the palm-tree winning-post well ahead of him.

'Now who's the winner?' said Tappo.

'I am,' said Monster, 'because you cheated.'

'*We* cheated? You're the one who cheated,' said Tappo.

'I'm not arguing,' said Monster. Then he opened his wide mouth, and gobbled up the three antelopes, GULP, just like that. 'I'm the winner,' he said, and there was no answer.

Another day, Monster was playing with some giraffes. There was an argument about who had the longest neck.

'Anyone can see,' said one giraffe, 'that our necks are the longest. No animal in the world has a neck as long as ours. It's our special point of beauty. You have a nice neck, Monster, but it's quite short.'

'I'm not arguing,' said the Monster. Then he opened wide his enormous mouth, and gobbled up the giraffes, all six of them, GULP, just like that.

'My neck is the longest,' he said and there was no answer.

Things became worse and worse. Sooner or later, Monster quarrelled with everyone. He gobbled up all the monkeys, the hippopotami, the ostriches, the elephants, the snakes, the lizards, the lions, the tigers and the baboons.

Now Mother Monster and Father Monster noticed what was happening, and they didn't like it at all.

'You shouldn't gobble up all your playmates,' said Mother Monster, 'even if you are a monster. Even monsters need someone to play with, and someone to talk to.'

'Nonsense,' said Monster.

'Don't talk to me like that,' said Mother

Monster, 'or I'll have to give you a smack.' (She had not noticed how big her Monster had grown.)

Monster just said, 'Oh no you won't give me a smack. And I'm not arguing with you, either.' Then he opened his terrible mouth and gobbled up Mother Monster, GULP, just like that.

'I'll gobble who I like,' he said, and there was no answer.

But Father Monster saw what had happened and he came running to give Monster the first and best smacking of his life.

'Oh no you don't,' said Monster, and he opened his cavelike mouth, and gobbled up Father Monster, GULP, just like that.

'I'll do just what I like,' he said. 'I'll gobble up who I like, when I like, *so there*,' and there was no reply.

The next day, Monster gobbled up all the crocodiles, the alligators, the birds, the gorillas, the leopards, the cheetahs, the sloths and the bears. By the end of the week, he had gobbled up every creature on his island.

'Now I'm the master of all the world!' he shouted. There was no reply. 'I'm the strongest, the fastest, the best, of all creatures,' he bellowed. There was no reply. Monster went to sleep, feeling well pleased with himself.

Next morning, forgetting what he had done, Monster woke up, and bellowed, 'Come and play with me!' There was no reply. Louder still he shouted. 'Come and play with me! I want someone to play with! Come out at once, or I'll gobble you all up!' Silence. Nothing moved. Then, 'Oh,' he said. 'Oh, dear, I had quite forgotten. I *have* gobbled you up. All of you. Who will I play with now?'

Suddenly, Monster felt a deep sadness inside him. For the first time in his life, he began to cry. He cried all day and cried himself to sleep when night came again.

As the days went by, Monster became thinner and thinner. He was too sad to eat, too sad to play, too sad to live.

'What's the use of being the only creature alive in all the world?' he said. 'I wish I could gobble myself up.' But that was one thing he could not gobble up. So he lay down on the beach, and ate nothing at all, and hoped he would soon die of hunger.

What Monster did not know was that his island was not the whole world at all, but only a tiny part of it. There were many other lands out of sight across the sea, all of them teeming with animals. So Monster was surprised when, as he lay upon the beach too weak to move, a dolphin came swimming up to him.

'Hello, what's wrong with you?' asked Dolphin. 'What a funny beast you are. Are you ill? Can I help?'

'You must be a dream,' said Monster, weakly. 'I've eaten everybody in all the world.'

'You look very thin on it,' said the dolphin. 'Anyway, you haven't eaten me, or the whales, or the fish, or the porpoises, I've just seen millions of them. There's more to the world than this little island, you know. Much more. There are hundreds of islands, most of them bigger than this one, and bigger places, too.'

Then the dolphin told Monster all about the

world and Monster began to cheer up. He told the dolphin his story, and why he was so lonely that he wanted to die.

So the dolphin said, 'I'll tell you what I'll do. I'll be your friend! But you must promise not to gobble me up, whatever happens.'

'Oh, I promise. I promise,' said Monster. 'I'll never gobble anyone up again. I'll eat coconuts, and leaves, and oranges.'

He kept his promise and the dolphin came to see him each day. He told Monster stories about the world and played with him in the shallow water. As the days passed, Monster grew slowly

stronger. Now that he had a friend, he no longer wanted to die, and he had come to like living on fruits, and leaves, and the roots he dug from the ground.

One day, he said to the dolphin, 'If you know anyone who would like to come and live here, it would be quite safe for them, now.'

'I'll pass the word round,' said the Dolphin.

So, quite soon, a whole family of alligators arrived on Monster's island and they quickly made friends. Then some crocodiles came, and some swimming snakes. A flock of birds flying over, came down to rest, and stayed to live on the island. Little by little, life came back to the island. Monster made friends with every creature, and there was no one more kind and gentle than he. He played with the little crocodiles, and let them climb over his back. He allowed the little alligators to pull his tail and tweak his toes in fun. Monster was happy again. But all the animals said, 'How strange it is that such a big strong animal should be so kind and gentle.'

The dolphin smiled to himself, when he heard this, but he kept Monster's secret, and said never a word about it.